ALL SMOKE RISES
MILK-BLOOD REDUX

by
MARK MATTHEWS

With an introduction by
KEALAN PATRICK BURKE

Wicked Run Press

"The wicked run when no one is chasing them"
Proverbs 28:1

Wicked Run Press

For more information, contact: WickedRunPress@gmail.com

Cover design by Zach McCain
Edited by Julie Hutchings
Introduction by Kealan Patrick Burke

BURNING QUESTIONS:
AN INTRODUCTION TO ALL SMOKE RISES

A READER ONCE ASKED ME if I thought it was possible to be a horror writer without experiencing any kind of emotional trauma. It was an interesting question and also, like most interesting questions, rather tough to answer. I *do* think it's possible to write horror without having had a hard life or any skeletons in the closet, but who among us is lucky enough to claim that we've never endured death, heartbreak, fear, or loss of some kind? I know plenty of horror writers who are jovial, happy people, many of whom had "perfect childhoods" (a description I am predisposed to find suspicious) and seemingly great lives. But life, by its very nature, trains us to be horror writers. The fears, anxieties, concerns that are waiting for you every time you open your eyes and prepare to face the day, are really all the tools you need to open a Word document and start to explore the dark corners of both your psyche and the world around you.

And if somehow, by some miracle you weren't raised by demons or suffocated by death and depression and your past contains no trace of dark blemishes that have stained your soul, well, you can still turn on the news and see how nightmarish life can be for people who are not quite so blessed.

As long as there are people, there will be horror, and those who feel compelled to analyze it. This leads to another question and one I get asked almost as often as the dreaded "Where do you get your ideas?" and that's: "In a world this fucked up, how can you justify writing horror?" The answer to this one, at least, is simple: "To understand it." With so much darkness and hate and violence and madness in the world, sometimes the only way to try to make sense of it is to personify it as a conquerable monster. We can't keep people from being massacred in Africa or Serbia or inside our own schools and movie theaters, but we can drive a stake through the heart of a vampire, vanquish a werewolf with a silver bullet, or lop off the head of a shambling zombie. It's horror we can control, even if that just means closing the book. It's a door we are *allowed* to close.

We have no such power over real life.

Which brings me to the book you hold in your hands now.

Mark Matthews' *All Smoke Rises* perfectly encapsulates horror as a reflection of real life.

When it was first released, some reviewers had difficulty with the subject matter—that of a child needing frequent injections of heroin to stay alive—and the fact that there are few, if any, sympathetic characters.

I find this somewhat baffling, and these are two of the novella's characteristics that most endeared me to it.

Horror fiction has *always* been most powerful when it subverts, subjugates and scrutinizes the predominant fears and anxieties of a given time period. In a way I found reminiscent of another suffocating and gloriously dark genre piece, Darren Aronofsky's film *Requiem for a Dream*, *All Smoke Rises* trains a cold, unwavering eye on addiction, the circumstances and desperation that lead to it, and the far-reaching consequences of that addiction. Is there any horror more devastating and tragic than the death of a child, or of a young girl being born into addiction and made to be its slave?

A few weeks ago, I saw a news story about a nine-year-old boy here in Columbus who suffers from the inescapable compulsion to scream, throw fits, and bite people whenever they get close to him. He can't concentrate when there is any kind of stimuli nearby, he cannot relate to people, even his parents, and he has to be medicated to sleep. And why? Because his mother took heroin when he was in utero. The child has a counselor, endures ongoing therapy, but it seems as if there is little that can be done to improve his condition. The boy was doomed before he was even born. He lives in a shitty, rundown neighborhood where low income families are shunted, only for it to become a no-go area when desperate people turn to crime to make ends meet. "Problem zones" the city calls them and it's exceedingly rare that anyone takes responsibility for the creation of those zones in the first place.

One of the things I loved most about *All Smoke Rises* is that—and this is the case with everything from *Frankenstein* to *Ringu*—the monster at the heart of the story is also the victim and as such we are horrified even as we are forced to understand and even sympathize with them. In Matthews' story, like that poor kid from Columbus, Lilly didn't ask to be born an addict, and now, emerged from the chrysalis of death, she has no choice but to feed on the tainted blood of others to keep the pain from tearing her asunder. Her condition is not presented as a metaphorical one, but that hardly dissuades the perceptive reader from divining plenty of subtext herein. Lily is her neighborhood, she is the cost of society's blind eye, the product of a failed system. Lily is the victim, a monster of our own creation. Children are so often at the mercy of their parents that it's impossible not to feel sympathy for the child, charred skin, dead eyes and homicidal henchmen notwithstanding. She is a product of her environment, of the careless decisions of others, her life shaped for her long before she was born. By us, because *we* are the true monster.

These are things everyone knows, but when it comes to the horrors of addiction, of poverty and the consequences of dubious choices, Mark Matthews may know more than most. Per his official bio, he is "a licensed professional counselor who has worked in mental health and substance abuse treatment for over 20 years". If you consider all that he must have seen and heard in those two decades, I think you'll agree that we are fortunate *All Smoke Rises* is short and *only* as horrifying as it is. And make no mistake, when it comes to citations of true horror, you'd be hard pressed to find a deeper and more challenging example than you will here. Matthews knows the heartbreak and tragedy of his subject. By the time you're done reading this, you will too, and that's something you *should* see, even if you don't want to, even if it makes you uncomfortable, and creeps under your skin like milk-blood.

Because that, too, is the definition of horror.

KEALAN PATRICK BURKE
Bram Stoker winning author of KIN
Columbus, Ohio
January 2016

Definition of MILK-BLOOD:
The act of extracting heroin-laden blood for reinjection at a later time. It usually is one's own blood, but could also be the blood of someone who has just overdosed. The term is used in Neil Young's 'The Needle and the Damage Done': "milk-blood to keep from running out."

"Hey little bird, fly away home. Your house is on fire, your child all alone."
~Tom Waits, (adapted from an English Nursery Rhyme)

ALL SMOKE RISES: MILK-BLOOD REDUX

IT ALL STARTS QUIET. Thick quiet, like cotton that fills up your ears so no sound can get in and all you hear are your own organs at work.

With all the women who work with you at Sharepoint Psychiatric hospital, you aren't often alone, but at that moment, you had the bathroom for your own private cavern. You stood with hands mounted on the sink and eyes staring at the mirror, taking in the sea of silence after a grueling week under the dark clouds of mental illness.

Streaks of grey were sprouting in your ponytail, barely noticeable in most lights, but the fluorescent bulbs of hospital hallways made the wiry strings glow like neon. You called them grey but they were really white, dead and lifeless, so that despite handfuls of Pantene conditioner, they were stiff as a corpse. When you started here as a psychiatrist seventeen years ago, the first black doctor the hospital had ever seen, there wasn't a sign of such aging.

The quiet moment ends when you hear the pounding of footsteps outside the bathroom door. A chase is underway. An army of staff members are bounding down the hallway and the familiar sound of a rugby scrum with a psychotic patient begins. A carpet-bombing of delusions and loose associations gush from the patient's mouth, and he wails like he is being burned at the stake.

A needle full of chemical restraints is surely on the way. *Shoot first and ask questions later*, was the mantra. After a five point takedown, a Haldol/Ativan cocktail will be injected into his skin.

You rinse your hands in the sink and dry them on your pants as you walk out the door.

Nurses and assistants are huddled around the man. His cheeks are scratched and blood splattered in tiny sprinkles. Psychotic screams fly from his mouth, none of his words decipherable, until his eyes make direct contact with yours, and then clarity strikes:

"You. You let him go," he screams into your face. "You did it. Now you must read and learn what happened."

A nurse has the syringe ready to fire. She plops it in, just a pin into a pin cushion, and his words stop. His muscles release and his eyes roll into the back of his head. His eyelids close and consciousness is gone.

"Self-serve walk-in," says the charge nurse. "Came on his own. Just another psychotic John Doe. Blood test for drugs is pending, but he has one big-ass oozing abscess on his arm from injecting something. Smells real bad. No cell, no ID, nobody he would let us call. All he had was a laptop bag full of papers, but no laptop."

It's 6:48 p.m. on a Friday, and you're done for the day. If they realize this John Doe has no insurance, he may get discharged pretty quick. If not, he'll be here when you come back on Monday.

Your drive home feels like one of those quiet moments in movies where the audience feels the main character reflecting. You do that once in a while: pretend you have an audience watching, one who would never reveal themselves, but who follow your life's drama. It helped with the loneliness. Your only marriage is to the pain of others, and the tears of the mentally ill have stained your soul. It used to feel heroic, but now you need cleansing.

It's an hour drive from the hospital to your two-bedroom house. You put your keys on the kitchen island, and look across your open floor plan out the front window. Your blood pumps faster than it should and your hand trembles a bit as you pour a glass of wine. Friday is a day harder to shake than the rest.

The damn breaks, just a bit, and you pound your fist on the kitchen island. A group of fruit flies rise into the air and circle over a plate of brown bananas. You watch the mass of tiny creatures scatter, fleeing in fear, their little brains no doubt wondering if it's safe to return to feast on the fruit. The bananas were bought when green, but ripened quite fast, and lie there like still-life, alone all day in this place you called home.

Where do fruit flies come from? you wonder. It's like they live inside bananas, buried in the yellow skin, only to be released to life when enough of the yellow decomposes into brown.

Two more glasses of wine in a dimly lit room and soon you're in your king-size bed. You pull the comforter under your chin and prepare for dreams you know will come. But there are no dreams that night, and you wake to a day of laundry, phone calls, and grocery shopping.

It was on Saturday night that the dreams came to you. Clients of the week rising from your subconscious, their bulging eyes, sad faces, beaten souls, bits and parts of all of them sewn together into one body. Limbs are twitching, mouths open, tongues wagging, waiting for you to give it pills like Zyprexa or Haldol.

When no pills come, the tongue returns to its mouth, the body gets a voice, and the lips whisper in your ear: *You. You let him go. You did it. Now you must read it and learn what happened.* You wake, the dream ends and the words stop. But each time you drift back to sleep the words are waiting there anew, each time with more energy, keeping you from full sleep, until finally an enormous bed-shaking crash of glass wakes you up completely.

Your heart machine-gun fires through your chest, and you shoot out of bed to the only window in your house that could have caused such a noise.

In the front room of your house, shards of glass from the shattered window covers the floor. A figure silhouetted against the faint light has stepped through and now stands in your house. A large bag is draped over his neck, and he moves like a midnight Santa.

His face is covered in shadow, but he stares straight at you as if he can see through the dark. You feel your heart pounding in your chest, and you're sure he can hear it, too. You need a weapon, you need to call for help, or you need to flee.

"What's wrong, good doctor?" he asks. "You always take your work home with you. Why so surprised?"

Your eyes adjust, reality gets stronger, and the voice hits your memory. It was John Doe, the psychotic John Doe from Sharepoint.

"They let me go," he tells you. "I didn't escape. They let me go. I told them I was okay, wasn't going to hurt myself, so they let me go."

"How. How did you know where I live?"

"Don't you understand? I have magic in my veins. I know things, I hear things. Things I wish I didn't. I even know what you'll do with Lilly. How you'll fix things after you did what you did."

The John Doe was discharged from the hospital too early, for his psychosis is still clear. He is full of nervous twitches, tiny motions and electric energy. He shifts his weight, swings the huge hockey bag off his neck, and plops it on the kitchen island. It lands with a thud. More fruit flies scatter in the air.

You need to either escape or talk him down. *Shoot first and ask questions later*, doesn't work without a Haldol cocktail to inject. It's fight, flee, or negotiate. Get into his mind, align yourself with him, then get him back to Sharepoint.

The man reaches into the bag, pulls out a pile of wrinkled papers, and sets them on the island. They sit under your nose, at least a hundred typed pages, and you begin a therapy session that may save your life.

"Is this something you wrote?" you ask, tapping the mound of papers.

"Yes. My second novel written about her. Started out as fiction, but it's true, it's not fiction. It's real. You'll see."

"And why did you bring the papers here?"

"Because, doctor, you must read it. And you must believe it to be true. I will show you that it is true. The real truth might burn your eyes right out."

"What is the story about?" You ask while thinking of your next move. If you even made it to the phone, it would be twenty minutes before the police would arrive. Or you could grab a knife from the kitchen. With your open floor plan, the butcher block wasn't far.

"A girl born of the streets of Detroit, living at 608 Brentwood. She lived with her grandma who some thought was a witch, and a man who tried to raise her, but he had no fucking clue. A mentally ill squatter who lived across the street was her real dad, but that was a secret. Every God-given thing about her was defective, and her gut was always hungry. Her mother was murdered, buried across the street, but the mother's spirit is powerful, and still haunts the girl to this day."

With each word, the man gets closer. Hurt sweats from his pores.

"I feel your sadness for this girl," you assure him. "Girls like her are the kind of people I try to help at the hospital."

"The hospital!" he laughs. "The hospital isn't real. It's a fortress made of brick and mortar and keeps real things *out*. It isn't the real world. You want to know how a lion lives, how he feeds? Visit the jungle, not the zoo. It's what I did. Been around a bit, been a social worker myself, Doctor."

You hear his claim of being a social worker, but dismiss it as the grandiosity of a psychotic.

"Doctor, how many people have you helped only for them to suffer longer? How many ghouls, how many rotten souls have crawled up from out of the Detroit sewer, spent a few days getting drugs from you at the hospital, only to return to the streets? You don't help them, you feed them and street them."

This isn't working. You eye the knife, you eye the front door, you think about his weak spots. His eyes, his neck, his crotch.

"In your story, does anybody help the girl?" you ask to buy time.

"If you count her uncle shooting heroin into her big blue veins to take away her pain. Changed her forever. Soon enough she needed heroin to exist… and then the night of the fire. The night of the fire, when the blood of all of them, all of them, her grandmother, her father, the psychotic monster, the bones of her mother, all of them were mixed in the bathtub, dripped into the basement where she was trapped. She injected the mixture into her own veins right before the place caught fire. It exploded her into something new. I went to visit and saw her."

"Saw who?"

"Lilly. I visited Brentwood and found her as I feared. Living in the abandoned house, days after the fire. She injected part of herself right into me. Look right here."

He points toward the black abscess in his arm and you lean in to look. It's a few weeks old but certainly not healing. It looks like someone put a burning cigar out on his arm.

"Lilly was in me, and I tried to help her."

"And did you?"

"No, I failed. I wanted to help her. To do something. To help her, or to help Oscar, the boy who died in a fire years before her. I failed. What could I do? I can't pretend to know. So all I did was follow her everywhere. Tracked her every move from afar. Not sure if she noticed me."

He's lost in his illusion, but you need to stay there with him. It's the only way he'll trust you. The only way to get him out of here. In the weeks to follow, you'll get a home security system installed, and you'll buy that dog you've been thinking of.

"Doctor," he asks, reading your thoughts. "You don't trust me. You don't believe me, do you?"

"I believe you are hurt by all of this. Really hurt, and I want to help you."

"Promise?"

"Promise."

That one word sets him in motion and he unzips the hockey bag with excitement. Whatever treasure is inside, he wants you to see, and he becomes an eight-year-old boy showing his mother his artwork.

When you see what's inside, however, you are not proud. Your stomach feels wretched and you gasp so loud you're sure he's offended.

A black skeleton. Or not a skeleton, but the skinny body of a child. He cradles the body in his arms like a doctor who's just delivered, and places it back down on the kitchen island.

"This is the body of Lilly".

Lilly was anything but a white flower. Her skin had been blackened and burnt. Charred legs and arms stuck out like tiny tree limbs, the knuckles on her fingers barely covered by skin. The child's face is frozen in the beginnings of a scream. She seems ancient as a mummy, but has on boy clothes that were fresh. The stench of singed hair burns the inside of your nose.

"She is yours to take care of. She suffers like you won't believe. I've got a tiny part of her inside me, but I can't take it anymore. I can't. Only thing I can do is to make myself die."

As if he'd been listening to your plans, John Doe dashes to the butcher block and pulls out a knife. The largest of them all. He waves it in his hand, moving like a spastic, psychotic house troll. You're losing him.

"Let me help you," you tell him. "I can help you. Tell me what happened? Tell me about her. Let me hear it, I want to know. Tell me your name, tell me what I can do for you."

"We are beyond that, Doctor. I'll not be able to live any longer. It was too much. Thought I could help her, but it's too much. She wants to be dead. You would want us both dead if you knew."

"No, I would not!" you scream. You wish the light would show the sincerity on your face. You think of tackling him. He reads your mind and points the knife at your face, freezing you on the spot.

"Knives like this," he says as he studies it. "It's like they're made for veins. You might think a razor to the wrists works best, but a knife slices better than the tiny blades."

He holds it at different angles, admiring it, feeling its weight.

"When I'm done bleeding out," he tells you, "before you do anything. Before you call anyone. Before you touch the body of Lilly. Read the pages. Read them through. Because you must."

You've never witnessed a suicide before, only seen them in dreams and heard of their details, but you are about to see your first. You thought it would be more somber, but that's not the case.

The violence is striking when John Doe begins slashing himself. First he slides the knife across his wrists, carefully, as if carving a turkey, but soon after he starts hacking away, nearly severing his hand. Blood comes forth like a fire hydrant's cap has been loosened on a hot summer day in the city.

After he falls to the ground and you're sure he's dead, he raises the knife one last time and slices across his neck.

Jugular cut. Fire hydrant completely busted open

The smell of blood coats the inside of your nose. The air becomes moist and humid. You kneel next to him, the sticky pool soaking your cotton PJs. Your hands get bloody, as if you were the one who did the butchering. His life is gone, and if his soul has risen, it's gone right through your own body on its way to where all souls rise.

The chaos is swallowed by the quiet. You sit in the silence, not wanting to move forward in time, for whatever is up ahead has changed too much. So you wait, but nothing. Even with the growing puddle of blood on your floor, there's a peaceful stillness to the John Doe that you didn't think he could find. You envied it. You wished it for all your clients.

You rise up from the ground. It's time to call 911. First responders will come, you'll speak to them as little as possible, and when they leave you'll crawl back into that shell of yours. Realtors will be contacted and your house will be put up for sale.

The plastic phone in your hand feels solid and safe. Just three digits, and then the authorities will come and take care of things. The dead body on the ground, and the body on your kitchen island, both will be taken.

You can explain the John Doe, but not the girl. Where did this girl he called Lilly come from? She seems frozen, not in ice, but in ash. Her face is stuck in pain and suffering, her eyes squeezed shut. Her burnt skin seems old and weathered, spread tightly across her youthful face and pug nose. Her cheeks are hallowed, her hair matted. You trace a finger along her bony arm—it's cold, but not frigid. Limbs stick out her jean shorts like a disfigured tree. Her blue t-shirt is the only thing that seems fresh.

Time to dial 911.

Before you do anything. Read this. Read it through. Because you must.

Who knows where he found her, if maybe he killed her himself and somehow kept her preserved. But why did he bring her to you? This was sinister beyond any tale that you've ever heard.

Next to her, lie the papers. The manuscript.

Your bloody thumbprint stamps the papers as soon as you pick them up, and the white manuscript is now as stained as your own soul.

And you read. *Because you must.*

ALL SMOKE RISES

CHAPTER ONE:
OSCAR'S MOM AT THE PAROLE OFFICE

PAROLE AGENT HASTINGS HAD A PIERCE THAT DIDN'T CRACK. The agent was a legend in the waiting room, and the stories flowed freely among the parolees about the beastly woman. Some say she used to be a prison guard but was forced to office work after an assault left an inmate paralyzed. The story changed on who assaulted who. Others said Hastings was a lesbian who hated attractive women. Some said she had a colostomy bag. Others said she had a prosthesis and that's why she limped. One person talked about the day she maced a parolee in her office for refusing to spit out their gum.

Not all of them could be true. Only thing Crystal knew for sure: Agent Hastings would be happy to have her locked back up again.

Crystal could see it all over her round, smooshed-in face. It was that of a hobgoblin who might attack at any moment with a billy-club. Siamese cat eyes swirled and penetrated with rays of judgment.

Crystal had to wait two hours to get called into Hastings's office, where she sat in a sunken chair while the goblin towered over her and interrogated. A felon's time doesn't count.

"Any change of address, Ms. Roundtree?" Hastings asked.

"No, no change, still on Hubbard Drive."

"No arrests or police contact since your last report?"

Crystal shook her head *no,* and was surprised Hastings didn't make her speak rather than nod, the way she often did.

"Not caretaking for any children?"

"No, none."

"Are you associating with other felons?"

"No ma'am. Just staying at my mom's. She's elderly, needs my help. As you know."

Agent Hastings typed the answers between grunts, and Crystal tried to decipher what she was writing by the tone of her keystrokes. Memos from judges and prosecutors were tacked to her bulletin board. Two sets of files were stacked up on the floor, and Crystal imagined one pile was for parole violators who would be having their date with the judge. The others were free to go and fight another day. Staying on the right pile seemed harder each week.

Nobody would care that Agent Hastings was a bitch of monstrous proportions, that she made you want to leave this office, find some crack-seeking punk and smash their head in for the twenty dollars in their wallet. Just because.

"You haven't got a job yet, Ms. Roundtree. You're in violation."

Violation. Hastings swung the word around like a battle axe.

"I do have a job, I work for cash four days a week. I'm doing hair freestyle, some nails, braids. I have a steady client list. People love my work."

"You need a job with a paycheck, and a boss, or someone I can call. It's in your parole orders." Hastings leaned forward and Crystal knew she didn't want to hear a comeback but gave one anyway.

"You want me to quit my job?"

Five years in prison for child endangerment, but guilty forever. She did five years and was released, but here she was, still sitting in front of a prison guard. Crystal thought about getting in her car, scooping up all the money she'd been tucking away, and going to California. Nobody would find her.

"I want you to get a job, not just cash. I need you to follow orders. The cash could be coming from anywhere. The judge didn't say you need to have *cash*, he said you need to have a job. Unless you can prove it with a paycheck, you do not have a job. Your choice on how to proceed, but if you come back here next week without a paycheck, you'll be in violation and have to explain yourself to Judge Donaldson"

Judge Donaldson. Last time Crystal saw him was at sentencing, through a stream of tears as she begged for leniency. It wasn't an act, but it was desperate. Donaldson gave her less than the maximum but said if he ever saw her again he would not be so kind. He hoped that her five years in prison would help her realize how her *gross negligence* had killed her son, Oscar.

Each time Crystal walked out the front door of the parole building, it felt like another release from jail. Each week was a desperate war she had to win, and if she lost, she'd be in violation. Before driving home, she trapped herself in the stuffy air of her car, lit up a cigarette, and inhaled. One huff, two, each time taking in more smoke and holding it in her lungs, hoping it would scald and burn. Hoping the smoke brought with it fire.

When the cigarette was down to the filter, she stuffed it in the overfull ashtray and drove off.

She went eighty-five down the Davison Freeway and her head filled with angry pressure. Her car rattled and she cursed the gas gauge that was down to zero.

Never enough cigarettes, never enough gas. Always down to zero.

She thought about going by her mom's house and making sure the set-up looked right. She remembered hearing a story about Agent Hastings doing one of her surprise home visits right on the scheduled report day, but that seemed like bullshit.

She looked in the rearview mirror. No sign of followers.

Maybe she should go to her mom's house anyway. She needed another pep talk.

Mom, my parole agent will stop by here, they will call. Just tell them I live here, okay? It's important that you say I live here. My stuff is here, but I'll be gone a lot. My agent will try to get you to lie. She will try to put me in jail. I'll make sure you take your meds, and help you with your oxygen tank, but I have to keep going to my cosmetology classes so I won't be here all the time.

Mom thought she was still in beauty school, but that lie wouldn't stick forever.

You don't need to have cash, you need to have a job.

It was a full-time job trying to keep Hastings off her ass and stay out of jail. Every time she saw a cop car, she thought she was getting arrested on the spot. Every week she had to hope Avanti wouldn't do something stupid and get raided. And every night she had nightmares of prison, waking each morning to the relief she wasn't still inside.

But not really free. She was marked up forever. Child endangerment charges were tattooed on her insides. Branded like cattle.

Go home to mom's house where it's safe. Where you have always been loved.

She blew past the exit to her mom's and went on to Brentwood .

Owl's Party Store was on the corner, and the same three men were there, drinking malt liquor in the handicapped parking spot. Next to Owl's was an empty lot with grass growing so high it splintered into wheat, the shambles of a house barely hidden beneath. Three boys were playing in the field using sticks as swords, and Crystal knew soon enough one of the boys would have his cheek cut up by an errant branch. He'd go home bloody and crying to a mom too busy to care for him.

That's why we need to keep our children inside. That's why we put locks on their bedroom doors. Because they walk out at night when they shouldn't. We need to keep them safe.

Empty lots. Empty houses. The street hadn't changed much in her five years being in prison, just more of the same. Her old house was falling apart and sinking into the ground. Something underneath was sucking it down, each day another piece crumbling. The city had boarded up the doors and windows long ago, but soon enough the boards were tagged with graffiti and then torn right off.

The house was Oscar's tombstone, his gravesite. Crystal stared into its soul every day, and the big dormer window on the second story stared back.

Crystal parked on the street and unscrewed her license plate to take it inside. License plates with legal tabs were golden around here and stolen all the time. All it took was a Philips head screwdriver and three minutes. Getting stopped for no-plates was a parole violation and a sure bet to land her back in front of Judge Donaldson. She was on top of her game and would take her plate inside.

The sidewalks were quiet and empty, but on the street a Ford Explorer was creeping by with two men in front. A white man in the driver's seat rolled down the window. His brow was sweaty and he frantically gnawed at his fingernails. Crystal recognized him and the passenger.

"Should we knock on the door as usual, or you want us to stay here?" he asked.

"What you want?"

"Oxy's or Vics. My friend wants heroin."

"Park down the street and wait until I'm inside. Park on the right, not the left," she added, just to let them know these were her rules, this was her neighborhood, and she was the queen to Avanti's king.

She went inside. The front room was empty but music came from the back. A sliver of light spilled into the hallway, and she heard Avanti's voice shout out:

"What did the parole lady say today? Did you tell her? Did you tell her you're moving so she'd have to transfer your ass somewhere else?"

"You know she won't approve the transfer. I'm stuck with her until I'm done. She's asking me for a paycheck. Doesn't matter I'm paying supervision fees and restitution. Says if I don't have a paycheck I'll have to talk to Donaldson."

"Sounds like a set-up to me."

"Where am I going to get a paycheck?"

"Well, I know how to take care of that. We can make it okay. I got a guy. But it ain't coming for free."

Crystal wanted him to hold her when he said he'd make it okay, but it was never like that with him, but at least Avanti understood. He'd been off paper for years and had nobody to report to. He was the closest thing to Oscar's dad that Crystal could find.

"There's two guys out front looking to buy, told them to wait. They'll be knocking in a second."

She went to the kitchen for leftovers from yesterday's meal. Meatloaf with thick gravy. She would wash it down with a Dr. Pepper, smoke a joint, and be completely content.

The frost of the refrigerator cooled her face, and there it was. Deep red sauce and meat that would be even juicier today after a quick zap in the microwave. Plus potatoes. All of it showered with pepper.

A knock at the door, soft and hesitant. Avanti moved to the front window where a blue blanket was spread about and acted as a curtain. He slid it to the side, undid the four dead bolts, then opened the door with gun in hand.

The two stepped through in a shroud of shame. The small kid was trembling and sweating so hard it seemed his head might burst if he didn't get an OxyContin soon. He was chewing on his fingernails like a drumstick.

The other guy, the driver, was big and maybe even pretended he was the muscle of the two, but came by every day and gave them thirty bucks. Three packs of heroin were plunged through the thick meat of his arms. Someday soon he'd ask for more, or would be broke and ask to be fronted. Or hell forbid, try to rob Avanti, which happened before but Vanti knew how to fire back.

Today he looked better than usual. Not the kid, who was tore up, pale as a corpse, and thirsty for some pills.

"No pills today. Sorry. Completely dry," Avanti explained and Crystal knew he was lying. "But you want me to fix you up with some dope? I can. You're wasting your money buying these pills anyway. Let me fix you up with some heroin. It's sad for me to see you this way. Let me do it, let me help you, for free."

Crystal felt the kid's stomach churning, each cell in his body screaming in need. No way would he refuse, and soon enough, both customers were boiling up some heroin to shoot. The young kid looked away when Avanti injected his arm with the syringe. Wasn't long before the sound of him vomiting was echoing off the bathroom tiles. He came out wiping the bile off his lips, but his shakes were gone, his walk steady, and he was high as fuck.

"You want this open or closed?" the happy little skeleton asked as he was leaving out the front door.

Crystal couldn't do anything but shake her head and watch the kid hop off the porch like a schoolgirl. She closed the door and he was gone, but his soul, his life, his whole world was now trapped inside. They had him now. Wherever he went, a long, unseen chain was attached to draw him back. All because of the tiny pinhole in his arm.

Crystal went to lie in bed and sucked down a joint, staring at the ceiling. She blew the sweet smoke in the air and watched it rise, thinking of the poor kid's mom. Her son was slowly dying now, just like her own son, Oscar.

The night went on, customers kept knocking, Avanti took care of them, and Crystal stayed in bed through it all, the earth spinning beneath her, and somehow she was still on it.

After the shades grew dark and traffic died down, Crystal went outside to the front porch to peer across the street at her old house. She did this many nights, smoking a cigarette and imagining it was seven years ago, and a burning Molotov cocktail was being thrown through the front window.

She could say she came back to Brentwood for her revenge. To kill the man who burned down the house and killed her child, but the legendary Zach Golson was found dead. Murdered in his house, which was then set on fire, killing his own child. Karma came back to him. His child was burned so bad, some say they didn't find her body but had to test the pile of bones and ash for her DNA.

Children don't escape here.

Crystal could still feel Oscar on this street. She saw him floating in the tiny dust particles in the air. She felt him inside every breath she took. Someday he'd come walking up to her and she'd give him a hug and never let go. His tiny body would crawl through the smoke, through the flames, out of his locked bedroom door, and they'd be together again.

You locked him inside his bedroom. That was gross negligence.

She smoked her cigarette and watched the nighttime darkness shade her old house, making shadows come alive. Waiting. Always waiting and watching for Oscar. And as she looked, she saw a small shape, crawling, just as she expected. Something was crawling out of her old house. A tiny figure moving slowly, lost, dying, it seemed, but not dead yet. He was reaching across the grass, pulling himself forward, trying to escape but too hurt to walk.

Oscar had finally escaped the fire.

CHAPTER TWO:
DWIGHT WALKS OUT THE DOOR AFTER HIS FIRST SHOT OF HEROIN

"YOU WANT THIS OPEN OR CLOSED?" Dwight asked the woman, but couldn't wait for an answer, for the weight of pain was lifted from his body and he bounced off the front porch. The tiny strings of his blue hoodie swayed with each step, the tips of his fingers still wet from chewing them raw. Big fat Brian at his side was just a safety blanket. A fluffy pillow to help cushion his trip down to Brentwood just before dark.

The fear of coming down here to score was long gone. Put out like a fire. All from the brown dust of an angel, or a devil, it did not matter which, but he knew soon as it was shot into his veins it was heavenly. Warmth spread about his body to the base of his brain. A sweet kiss to his spine. When he first felt the high, vomit had shot from his gut like the last waste of his old life, and now he was ready for something new.

The army of opiates swimming through his blood was stronger than ever before, ready to fight off the pain of life. First he had to bust out of this nasty street and get to his own neighborhood with trees and working street lights.

Dusk settled outside and the lone streetlight shone like the North Star in space. Houses full of shadows, some with bars on the windows, others with no doors on the front, but all of them ready to suck their victims inside. Each house alive with its own heartbeat, promises of secret happenings inside.

Dwight wanted no part of them. The darkness here couldn't invade the rainbow inside of his heart. All of his organs were smiling, life was okay. He finally knew his part, his purpose in the world.

Then out of the night it came. Brian was first.

A hand reached out of the darkness, grabbed Brian's head, and smashed it against the side of the Explorer. The metallic crunch was either Brian's skull or the crack of the car, Dwight was not sure which, but either way one of them was broken.

Then came the knife.

The beast sliced the knife from side to side, like a painter, each stroke making Brian scream in pain. The slashes kept coming, faster and faster, before the beast finally ended his masterpiece and plunged the knife straight into Brian's bulging gut. It stuck there like an exclamation point.

Brian fell to the ground and the dark monster peered over him, gave him a kick, picked up a large pipe from its side, and used it to beat Brian some more. The sound of metal on bone echoed through the indifferent street.

Once the monster was done with Brian, Dwight was sure he'd be next.

He grabbed the door handle and gave it a pull. Still locked. *You always lock it here.* His fingers tapped wildly at buttons on his keys. Hot breath of the beast clouded the air.

Too late to get in the car. Time to run.

Dwight heard a whistle in the air as the beast swung the pipe. His rib took the impact and snapped on contact. The meat in between felt it would drip from the bone. Dwight fell to the ground, curled into a ball, and waited for the next blow.

The pipe crashed down on his skull. With each smash, agony shot through his body and he could feel his brain being battered. Blood flowed. His vision hazy. Death was taking him, and the army of heroin had left him for this war.

One more blow and Dwight was sure his brain would completely shatter, but the beast stopped, sniffed something in the wind, and let its hands hang limp at his side.

"I got money. My family has money. My car. You can have it. Whatever you want," Dwight pleaded.

The beast shuffled his weight, walked two steps, turned, and started pacing back and forth. Dwight said a desperate prayer in his head; *God, get me home safely tonight, and I promise I will never use drugs again.*

The beast was a man, but didn't seem human. His neck was sliced open so deep that his head hung towards one side. Heat radiated from its body. Its face was twitching, lips moving as if speaking words, but they were too quiet and fast to hear. It yanked the knife out of Brian's gut, kept pacing, and finally spoke loud and clear.

"One's not enough. Need more. My girl needs more."

The beast raised the pipe in the air and started whaling on Dwight's leg, hammering away like an axe man chopping wood. The sound of Dwight's bone snapping was nearly as loud as his screams. He fell to the ground and his tibia busted through his skin. The monster grabbed him, dragged him over the grass, past the sidewalk, and up the porch to whatever torture awaited.

The house smelled like an old motel where smoke and sin were forever stuck in the walls. No lights were on, and the lone streetlight cast one ray through the busted boards on the window. Shadows of furniture were like dead men turned to stone, waiting to be awakened.

It wasn't long before Brian's body was dragged from the front lawn and laid right next to him. Dwight could see his face just inches way, pressed against the floor, and imagined whispering escape plans to him, telling him it would be okay.

But Brian was dead, and Dwight was just waiting his turn to be killed.

God, get me home safely tonight, and I promise I will never use drugs again.

The monster kept pacing about the room, in and out of the shadows, mumbling to himself. *Maybe he'll forget about me,* Dwight thought. The shadow seemed confused, like he lost his wallet or his thoughts and was moving about the house looking for it, until he finally disappeared behind a door. Dwight heard his heavy feet making fast steps down basement stairs.

Dwight was alone. Time to move. He tried to pull himself up, but his shin bone stabbed into his skin. He couldn't stand. Instead, he reached his hands out far as he could, and pulled himself forward, a few inches closer to the door. He'd dragged himself just two feet when the monster returned from the basement. Dwight couldn't help but cry, and tears mixed with the blood on his face. There was no escape.

"My girl. Needs what she needs," the beast said, carrying something in his arms. It came closer and Dwight saw what it was.

It was a doll. A life-size, disfigured doll that he'd been keeping in this abandoned home. The doll was laid over its arms the way a husband might carry his newlywed, and the beast gazed down at it with tenderness. It seemed like a burnt, plastic toy that had been pulled out of a fire. The tiny arms and feet swayed as the monster moved, side to side, and its face was so human.

The beast set the doll down on the sunken couch in front of them, brushed her hair from her eyes, and folded her arms over her chest. He even had her fingers interlocked. She looked like a cadaver, lying in state.

Then the beast knelt over Brian's body, turned his head side to side, and started dabbing his fingers in Brian's wounds.

"Too much of it spilled. Too much of it wasted. Ah, but it's good, some good milk-blood here. This man been doping for a long time. Long time."

"You ain't got this kind of dope in your body, my friend," the monster said to Dwight. "I'm starting with this one first."

It thwacked at Brian's neck with its fingertips, and then pulled a syringe from his pocket. He studied it at eye-level, like a nurse at a blood drive, aimed it at Brian's neck, then plunged it into his jugular. Moments later, it pulled back the plunger until it was full. Full of Brian's blood .

"I hear you thinking, I hear you breathing, I know what you're thinking, but you just aren't a daddy like I am. You don't understand. We do these things for our children. We father them, we mother them. We bring them what they need.

"You see, this is for my girl. My daughter. Ain't ever been a dad in history who will do what I do for this child. Uh-uh. Not my dad. Not your dad. Not my moms, not your moms. Not anyone's. You ain't seen such love. Good thing your eyes didn't close before you saw this."

The doll's face. It was so human. Perhaps not a doll at all, but a dead girl that the beast had killed long ago and kept around as a plaything. The beast treated it as such, and held up the arm of the skeletal creature, his fingers wrapped all the way around its wrists.

Then he poked the needle into the tiny arm.

Whatever the child was made of, it wasn't easy to inject, and Dwight remembered the prick of the metal in his own arm just hours before.

Shadows in the room started to change, tiny creaks of the baseboards became quiet, the dark of the room was sucked inside the syringe, all of it being siphoned into the girl's arm.

"There you go, my sweetness. It's good. It's good, isn't it?"

He laid her wrist gently back down on the couch, stared at it in worship, head cocked to the side in perpetual confusion. Waiting.

Like a marionette being pulled by strings from above, the child began to move.

First her head raised, just a touch, which would have seemed a trick of the shadows had it not been followed by her eyes opening. The whites of her pinhole eyes were framed by the charcoal skin of her face. With one feeble arm, she pushed herself up on the couch, and swung her stick legs to sit upright. Her head swirled to keep looking around the room, as if waking in some strange place. Finally, her eyes burned straight into Dwight with interest.

The doll was alive and gazing straight at him.

"This is my daughter, Lilly, and she needs more."

CHAPTER THREE:
LILLY WAKES UP

INSIDE THE SHELL WHERE I'M TRAPPED, it feels like tiny creatures made of fire are eating my organs, hallowing out my insides. Whatever is left running through my veins feels like burning razor chips, forever cutting, forever hurting.

And I lie in wait for Poppa to take the pain away.

Words of the dead speak to me. I hear my mother, my grandmother, and Oscar, all of them chattering for hours while I wait.

LILLY, COME WITH US. LILLY, YOU SHOULD BE HERE.

I listen, but I don't talk back. I never talk back. I just ache, burn, and the words are part of the flames that swirl inside of me.

I'm unable to lift my head or open my eyes, but I feel Poppa Jervis's fingertips wrap around my arm. His flesh is of my flesh, his sickness is much like mine. He taps a finger at my wrist, readying my veins for the prick of the needle.

Here it comes.

Ahhhh. So soothing when it shoots inside of me, filling my veins, rushing to my heart. The muscle responds with a beat and shoots the new blood everywhere. My body is brought back to life, and the sharp bits of cold barbwire ripping up my insides turn to warm baby blankets.

"There you go, my sweetness. It's good. It's good, isn't it?" said Poppa Jervis.

Energy returns, pain recedes, my eyes open and I see the trembling body of a man on the floor. His face is shredded, mangled, and his leg is twisted in an unnatural position. His pale skin is colored by blood and mixed with tears.

A dead boy is at his side. I see that Poppa cut him up. It's the dead man's blood that Poppa Jervis used to wake me from my sleep of pain.

"This is my daughter, Lilly, and she needs more," Poppa told the hurt man.

I did need more. I looked up at Poppa, the only one who would take away my hurt. A lullaby played in my head while I watched him move, and I hated myself for it. He didn't raise me, but it was his flesh, his sickness, that I was made of. He was the mother and father of my world now.

"Lift me up."

"Lift me up," Poppa mimicked me in soft words. I felt his cold, muscular arms on my tiny back as he set me on my feet.

Milk-blood swirled through me, gave me focus, and the voices that taunted me were gone. In front of me, the tiny man who Poppa Jervis hadn't yet killed was on the ground, trembling.

"How did you get here?" I asked.

His jaw hung slack, from fear or because it was smashed, I was not sure, but he started to crawl away furiously towards the front door. Poppa Jervis banged the pipe on the ground close to his head. He knew enough to stop, since his skull would be next if he kept moving.

"How did you get here?" I repeated, knowing he couldn't see well through the dark. He didn't have my ash-dark eyes, and I would have been just a shape in the shadows to him.

"Car," he answered in a tone as if he was speaking to the police. "My car. You can have it, and my money. You can have it all. Please, just let me go."

"That is not what I mean," I said.

Poppa Jervis was working on the fat man's dead body, trying to stick a syringe into his leg but missing his mark. He put a finger into the gobs of blood on the floor, then up to his nose and sniffed. He dabbed some on his tongue as he started working on another limb. I knew it wasn't easy when the blood stopped circulating.

"I mean how did you get *here*? How did you get to the point that you wanted to be here on this street? At this hour?"

He couldn't respond. His head bobbed as he cried silently. Mucus and blood made tiny bubbles out of his nostrils. I remembered tears like this. Tears I had as a child that I learned soon enough didn't do a thing.

"You have a hurt to fix, don't you?" I said as much as asked. "You go looking to fix that here, you find more hurt, you become hurt, you hurt others."

Poppa Jervis finally had a syringe full of new blood. I turned my arm to its underside to help him find a spot, but instead he had his hands at my neck, just under my chin. *Ahhhhhhh...* another plunge, right into the sweet spot, where Daddy Zachary used to tickle me, back when my skin was soft with a blue tint from cyanosis and I had warm, live blood cells rushing wild.

Days ago I would have refused blood from a newly fallen addict. I'd hold off for straight heroin, but Poppa Jervis couldn't find much of that, and knocking on the dope-man's door doesn't work when you look like him or I. Heroin addicts also carried it in their bloodstream, and Jervis found them on the street and fed me their blood. I had no choice, for without it, I was stuck inside the sleep of pain. Each day this happened made me age, like I had lived the lives of every wretched person's blood put inside of me.

But this man in front of me was different from the others. I could smell his blood was fresh, full of life, full of hope. He wasn't yet tainted.

I didn't want him to die.

"Is it like that? You come here because you hurt? How did you get here?" I asked again.

"Someone gave me pills," he finally answered. "I took them. Just pills. I kept taking them, then I started needing them. I never did any heroin until tonight. That guy across the street gave it to me for free. I'm not like this. I'm going to college. I'm not part of here…"

No, he wasn't. Not yet. But soon enough, this street would rip apart his rib cage and stick a hand through his sternum, grab a hold of his heart, and turn him inside out. He'd had his first taste, and his insides will ache for more.

I knew he would ache for it because I had the same kind of ache. Soon after Uncle Nelson had put the needle into my veins I craved heroin. The man who did this to me, my uncle Nelson, was living across the street like nothing happened.

How can Uncle Nelson just live on like nothing happened while I suffer like this?

So many nights I spent sitting as a shadow on the front porch, watching lights go on and off in Uncle Nelson's home. I knew that certain lights going out meant Joey was asleep. I knew that my auntie had to care for Nelson since his diabetic foot had been amputated. But it didn't stop him from getting high. Many people go in and out of his house, staying long enough to deliver dope.

The day he put the needle into my veins changed my life forever. I was so tiny, but with big fear and big veins. His skin was like sandpaper against my own flesh when he touched my arm to shoot me up. Then I kept going back to him, listening to him say how people like me don't deserve mothers that care for them. That heroin was the only cure for my sickness.

It turned out, he was right. And now Jervis kept killing people to help me. Soon enough, he'd kill this man who sat before me. Another one dead, this one innocent, while Uncle Nelson just sat in his chair across the street and watched TV. This night he was alone, for Auntie was gone with Baby Joey at her side.

Jervis aimed the third shot of dope at my foot, ready to inject.

"Save it," I said. "Save it and fetch him, fetch him for me now, Poppa. Go fetch Uncle Nelson, like we talked about."

Poppa Jervis laid the needle down next to me. His face twitched, and then he raised the long, stained knife that swayed by his side and picked at the gash in his neck.

Fetch him, Fetch him now. Poppa Jervis repeated my commands and started his walk. His boots stomped out the door, and he was swallowed up by the darkness outside.

The man on the ground looked at me, wondering if it was safe or if I was going to hurt him. He was terrified of me, where just a short while ago, he wouldn't have noticed me. He would have ignored the bruises on my arms and my skinny belly that school lunches and moldy bread couldn't keep full. I'd become so thin I was nearly invisible.

But now I was terrifying. My skin was an armor of dark charcoal. My eyes were like white flames that burned. My finger reached out to touch his cheek. It was smooth. Fresh. The suburbia air had preserved it like a fetus in formaldehyde.

"Imagine what it's like to be born here."

He was listening to me now, with full attention.

"My mom, she was assaulted too, by the very man who cut up your face. That's what got her pregnant. She didn't want me, she knew I wasn't right when I was in her belly, but I was born anyway, my heart as defective as your face. My pops—the man who thought he was my pops at least—he took care of me. My mom wanted me killed so instead he killed her and buried her on this street. Thought it would help. Just made things worse. She still haunts my insides."

"I'm sorry," the man said. "Maybe I can help you..."

"*Maybe you can help*," I mocked. "Folks like you been trying to help me for a long time. Social workers, writers, they can't do it. They run for help themselves when it gets too deep. Last person who tried to help was a white man like you. I injected parts of me right inside him to help him understand, but it blew up his mind instead. He wanted to help me, to help Oscar, but it was too much."

"Just let me go, please," he pleaded.

Under the dirt and blood there still glowed a life inside this man that tried to shine through. When Papa Jervis came back, he'd dig back into this man and soon he'd be dead.

If I hadn't sent Poppa Jervis away, he'd be dead already.

"What would you do if you left?" I asked.

"I would never come back. Or I'd send you money if you wanted it. I would do whatever you wanted. I just don't want to die."

The pant of his breath was like a dog's, and it smelled of fear.

"Go then. If you can move, then get out of here. If it's really true that you're not from here, then you can leave here. If you can't make it? Well, then I guess you're here forever."

The man reached out with one hand, then two, and began dragging himself across the floor. A trail of blood followed him. Another reach, another drag. One of his legs kicked forward, but the other was dead weight.

I waited until he made it out the door, and then retreated to the back bedroom with the syringe full of blood Poppa had saved in my hand. I dreamed that someday I would have a million syringes full of milk-blood saved up and I wouldn't need anybody's help ever again.

I laid down on the springs of the burnt-out bed in Oscar's old bedroom and looked up at the ceiling. I heard thumping noises; *boom, boom, boom,* but it was just the man's body banging and crawling down the front porch steps. He'd have to work hard to get back to his own world, but he'd make it if he wanted it enough.

I just don't want to die. His last words echoed in my head.

You just don't want to die, but I do. I do.

CHAPTER FOUR:
CRYSTAL WATCHES THE BODY CRAWLING ACROSS THE STREET

CRYSTAL EXHALED CIGARETTE SMOKE INTO THE AIR, watched it disappear, and waited for the crawling body across the street to disappear just the same. The vision was just a trick of the night on her mind. Something she had hoped to see years ago.

Now it was mocking her.

This was not Oscar, but a waking dream. Like the dreams she had where he spoke to her. Or the nightmares of him trapped in his bedroom, crying out for help, flames outside the door, smoke seeping in through the cracks. Maybe blaming her, maybe hating her with his last thoughts.

What was he thinking just before he died?

The image of the crawling body remained. She kept watching.

It was no illusion.

It did not disappear, but moved like a half-smashed insect crawling for safety. This is what Oscar would have looked like had he busted out of the locked door of his bedroom and escaped the flames.

This was Oscar.

She tapped the cigarette out, heart pulsing hard. Two steps, three steps, across the lawn, sprinting by the time she hit the street, and in seconds, she stood over the crawling person. This was no child, but a man. Skinny, bloody, beaten. The pain came off of him like heat. Someone had beaten the living shit out of him, and left him for dead. Well, he wasn't dead yet.

The man's neck craned to look up at her, and she realized it was her customer from earlier that night. Shot up his first pack of dope and then never made it out of the neighborhood. There he was, trembling and tore apart.

"Help me, please," he asked through gurgles. "Call 911. I need an ambulance."

Her fingers moved to her cell in her pocket, gave it a pat, but stopped there. She would not call 911. Police would come—maybe take them an hour, but they would come—and they'd question her, run her name, see her status, contact Agent Hastings. She'd kill this man before she'd let that happen.

What the hell did happen to him?

She turned to go home and leave him, but that was risky. If he was found like this, alive, he'd say where he got the dope. Then she'd be questioned anyways. She needed him gone.

There, on the street, she saw his destination. The purple Ford Explorer.

"I'll stick you in your car," she said, and bent down to pick him up.

"No." He grunted in pain for her to stop, then yelped like a dog after she lifted him. He hopped to the car with her help, yelping louder with each step. She opened the front door of his car and dropped him in the seat. He was a mess. One eye swollen shut, legs smashed apart, his hands trembled on the steering wheel.

"I don't care how messed up your face is. Drive the fuck out of here. Don't say where you were. Don't say where you got anything. You didn't get it from me."

The Explorer made it down the street, the red brake lights like the eyes of a snake, retreating to somewhere safer than here.

She turned back to look at her old house. The man's insides had left a trail from the front door, down the porch and through the grass. It all seemed quiet inside, but something had happened. The house does not give up its secrets easy, Crystal knew this, so she stared into the gaping doorway, deep as she could, watching and waiting while the house stared back. Nothing moved. Nothing seemed different.

She'd been inside the house more than once since she'd been back from prison. As soon as the boards on the windows and door had been torn off, she took a tour through the ghosts of her old memories. A drunken homeless man scrambled out with his bag of goods as she'd entered. She toured the house for an eternity, but left feeling let down, despite all the nights she'd imagined what it would be like to come back and bathe in the fumes of Oscar's remains.

She would go inside again tonight. Whatever and whoever might be in there, this was her house, this was Oscar's tombstone, and she was its guardian.

She walked up the stairs, bits of her old ceramic flower pots crunching under her feet. She took one step inside the black, open doorframe, and waited for her eyes to adjust. Waited for the house to remember who she was.

The couch where she and Oscar used to sit for hours was still there, moved to the side and charred from the fire. But next to it was something new.

A person.

Crystal tensed her leg, ready to kick, ready to claw. She'd fought off greater men than him before, but he didn't move. Everything was still and silent.

She took a step closer, and realized that this was not a living man, but a dead body. It was the other dope fiend from hours earlier, the one who'd bought three packs of dope, and whose friend had just crawled for help. This man here was not so fortunate to escape. Dark puddles pooled around him.

Who did this, and were they still inside?

The wooden floorboards creaked in agony. They were weakened by the fire, and felt ready to snap in half, dropping her in the basement below.

The scent of ash was in the air. With each breath, she took in Oscar. She inhaled deep in her lungs, and then exhaled, letting it float to the ceiling. She could still see him in this very spot, gazing up at her, waiting for permission to do something that she'd inevitably say no to. He was always curious about the world, ready to explore. Not a child who would be stuck living on Brentwood had he lived to adulthood. At least that's what Crystal had always dreamed.

Oscar, if you're here, give me a sign, she said in her mind, and then waited in stillness to hear a response. The house answered back in tiny creaks, mocking her, only significant in that they were the same as the ones before.

She took steps towards his bedroom, remembering the patter of his feet down this same hallway and then the sound he made behind his closed bedroom door. Especially after his window and door had been locked, he'd go inside and have a wild rumpus, jumping off the bed, having imaginary battles, setting up army men all about his room and then smashing them down like Godzilla. How she wished she'd never have gotten angry at him in these moments.

She remembered tucking him in at night underneath his Transformer bed sheet, sometimes stepping on a Lego and cussing under her breath, hopping on one foot trying not to disturb his sleep. Closing the door was done quietly, so as not to wake him, and then she'd set the padlock on the outside of his door frame.

Putting the nail in his coffin. Gross negligence. Killing her own son.

There was no trace of the lock she'd installed on his bedroom door. Firemen had smashed it apart. They'd smashed out all the windows, every door, before pulling Oscar's dead body out of his room. He was blackened, but not burnt. Died of asphyxiation from the smoke, so they said.

Crystal stepped inside and waited for her eyes to adjust to the darker pitch of black. Around the bed, rather than Legos, she saw used syringes. They lay upon a pile of soot next to an old box spring, still in the same spot, but no longer holding up a mattress.

And on the broken, filthy box spring, she saw another vision. The body of a child was lying there. A hallucination, born from the wishes of her own mind, she knew it, but she stood over it just the same. She was a mother again, watching her child sleep.

She could have stood there forever, until her own body was covered in soot and just as dirty as the floor. Until the city finally decided to tear this building down. Until this whole city imploded, she'd still be standing there, over a perfectly still child. To leave this room was to lose her illusion.

Then the child moved.

Like an infant, struggling and stretching against its limits to hold its head up to see its mother. First the neck, then a frail hand reached up to her.

"Oscar?"

Crystal reached down to touch the child's hand, held it softly, and stroked the skin. It was cool to the touch, cooler than it should have been, but the flesh warmed to hers immediately. The child's hair was matted, like deformed dreadlocks. Her skin was scaly, if that was skin, and it clung tight to her bones. The stench of burnt hair and flesh hung in the room like rotten incense.

"Oscar?" she asked again.

No words, but sounds. The child was trying to speak, perhaps, but the words were too weak to be understood. *How long had she been here?*

Crystal thought of calling 911 and then leaving, hoping an ambulance could take this child to a hospital and get her living again. But no doctor could help this child. It was too late for that. This was not normal. This was what happened when someone new grew from the ashes. This was the color when black was burned.

And this child was not Oscar

First off, it was a girl. Crystal could see it in the soft sadness of her feminine cheekbones. She ran a finger through the girl's hair and imagined the child's real mom had worked it over many times trying to get the hair to obey, but finally gave up and let it grow wild.

More soft noises came from the girl's mouth, and then her eyes opened. They glowed white in the dark room, and Crystal was staring straight into them. She realized who this was.

"I know who you are. You're Zach Golson's child."

"And I know who you are," the girl replied. "You're Oscar's mom. This was his room, where he slept. Where Oscar died."

The girl looked around the room as if tracing a fly.

"How?" Crystal asked. "How do you know these things?"

"Ashes," she said, and Crystal squeezed her hand.

"Ashes can talk to ashes."

"And is that what you are then. Ashes?"

The tiny black pupils, surrounded by snow white, were now wet with tears. She blinked once, and a puddle fell across her cheek. She blinked twice, and the tears went away.

"You can leave. You don't need to stay," the child said, and finally broke eye contact.

"I don't know that you're real. I don't know that this isn't a dream. I want to stay here. I will stay here. Until you go to sleep. That's what I did sometimes. With Oscar."

"Well, when I sleep, it isn't so nice."

"What do you mean?"

"I'm broken," the girl said, and then held up a syringe in her boney fingers. "This is the only thing that wakes me up."

Crystal took the syringe from her hand. The plastic felt slick and dirty. She tilted it side to side and saw it was full of fluid, maybe even blood.

"I cannot just leave another child in this room. I *will* take you."

She bent down to pick the girl up, held her close to her chest, and realized how frail she was. The body was all bone, and clung to her as if her own.

She carried the child through the doorway of the bedroom, the one that had been padlocked so many years ago, but now was barren, busted, and burned. She walked past the dead body in the front room. The fresh night air greeted them outside.

Crystal expected to see Agent Hastings standing on the front lawn, her troll-face grinning, a set of cops behind her with their tasers ready. *We know you've broken your parole orders and you're taking care of a child. We know you're selling dope. We've known all along. Now you're ours.*

Then they'd snatch her up and take her back to prison.

The dead body in the house would be found soon enough, or perhaps just as likely cleared by the person who killed him, but Crystal was walking out of there with a child in her arms, and it was what she'd wanted for the last ten years.

Crystal carried the child up and down Brentwood for a bit. Her flesh wasn't as warm as a baby's, certainly not as smooth, but it felt like it was all hers. She walked the sidewalks of the street, watching and waiting for someone to jump from the shadows, but the real danger was bringing her home to Avanti. That would be the scary part. If she told him this was Zach Golson's daughter, Avanti would rip her in two.

So Crystal pretended she didn't have to go home and kept walking under the black sky. Lilly looked around her with interest and wonder, and Crystal didn't stop until they both became tired.

"My eyes are closing, the dreams are coming, take me back," the girl whispered.

It was time to go home.

Crystal had not brought her keys, so had to knock at the front door and wait, while rocking the child back and forth. She saw Vanti peek out from behind the blue blanket over the window.

The bolts on the door unlocked.

CHAPTER FIVE:
JERVIS GOES TO FETCH UNCLE NELSON

"FETCH HIM, FETCH HIM NOW, POPPA."

Lilly's words fueled him across the street. Her voice filled up his empty head. That and the itch. The neck itch that always felt like tiny fire ants biting into him. Digging his knife into the itch made it go away. The day of the fire he sliced his own neck but never finished the job. Now his head hung at an angle, tilting and dangling. And always itching.

He loved Lilly in a new way ever since that day. Like an explosion inside his chest unveiled something new in both of them. She really became his daughter the night of the fire. Now he was always inside of her, like he was her heart, a broken defective heart, but the only one she had. He wouldn't let her stop living. Even when her eyes closed for so long, her black eyelids looking so at rest, he knew what to do to open them again. The smack. The milk-blood. He filled her up with what he could find, and then went for more.

Her skin was crusty but accepted the needle. Inside of her was something that took in the dope. His own skin was wrinkled, shriveled, but hers was a magnificent armor.

Sometimes he'd find a sharp, new syringe with the plastic still on the tip that would last for days, but when the sharpness dulled, he'd look for a dope fiend with works in his pockets. Rigs for the shooting.

Feeding her fed him. Bringing her dope was his mission.

No more words to recite inside his head, no more numbers to remember. The digits of his disability bank account were memories he needed for his old self, not for this new fatherhood.

He twisted the tip of the knife into his neck, grumbled in his chest, and heard the words of his girl again.

Fetch him, fetch him for me now, Poppa

Lilly wanted him to fetch Nelson, the man who first shot her up with heroin. She wanted him hurt. She didn't say so, but he knew it. He knew what Lilly needed. He could see it in the whites of her eyes, surrounded by the black color of her spirit.

Lilly was hurt by Nelson same way Jervis had been hurt by his dad. The way his daddy's eyes used to burn into him, the way his dad could just enter a room and make it go dark. It only got worse after his father died in jail. The voices got louder then, echoing in his ears, until the day he shot dad's ashes into his own skin. It exploded the voices inside like a firework, forever going off in his head.

How many days had he spent in jails, in psych hospitals, or locked in basements, tortured by the voice of his dad? *Jervis you're a devil, a red devil.* That was gone now. Now he had someone to love. Now he was a dad himself.

Jervis stepped onto the porch. It creaked under his boots. A soft light shone in the window. He spun the door handle but it was locked and wouldn't move. No bars on the window in this one. A quick kick with his boot and the front window smashed. Two more kicks and it shattered enough that he could step right through.

The air inside was still and silent, but each clop of his boots awoke noises. Piles of shoes lay near the door. A child's toys were scattered on a faded carpet. Somewhere inside this house there was dope, and lots of it. Jervis could smell it.

One lamp shone dimly in the next room, and Jervis followed. There was Uncle Nelson sitting in the recliner. The man was yellow, like a lightbulb glowing neon. His eyes were closed, and Jervis stood over him as he slept, or more likely had nodded off. The man smelled of old sweat, like Jervis's own dad. He put the knife up to Nelson's neck, and the man didn't flinch. A permanent snore rustled though his nose. His flesh hung saggy at his neck, like a turkey, waggling as he breathed. The jugular pumped blood just under the butcher knife, begging for Jervis to slice right across it.

But that would kill him too fast. *Fetch him,* Lilly had asked. She wanted him brought back. She wanted him to know what he had done to her.

Nelson's leg was cut off at the knee, amputated, and his pants were folded up and paper clipped together. Jervis thought of cutting his other leg off somehow. If he could saw right through the bone, he could leave the leg here and drag the man home. Or just smash it up real good and bust the bone in half, but he had no pipe, only the knife. He needed something to make the man hurt.

The bridge of his nose was thick, his eye cavities deep, and underneath the wrinkled eyelids, his pupil twitched. *His weak spot.* Jervis aimed his knife at one of Nelson's eyes. With a push he could poke one straight through, blind the man, and wake him up.

But before he could, Nelson's eyes popped open.

"I know you," Nelson said, unflinching, staring straight at the tip of the knife.

Jervis held the knife aimed at his iris long enough to make it clear he could have stabbed it straight into his brain if he'd wanted to. Nelson knew, but didn't blink, so Jervis pulled it away and itched the gash in his neck.

"You know me, eh? You know a lot then."

"Yes I do," Nelson said. "You think I don't know you?"

"I think you don't."

"I do. I knew you back when you lived like a motherfucking bum. Damn, you did some shit. I know. I saw you jump on Lilly's mom. Watched it. Saw her spill her bags of groceries. Saw you get all up on her, inject some sick part of yourself into her. I know you two made that deformed kid Lilly together. I know all of this. Who do you think carried Lilly's mom home after you jumped on her like that?"

Jervis traveled back to that moment. The mother of his child was dead and buried, but she'd spoken to him since then. She was strong.

"And," Nelson added, "I know, that YOU. Are the one. Who killed. My brother."

Jervis pulled the knife from the gash of his own neck, held the tip towards Nelson's face. The man's skin was just as faded as the leather of the chair he sat in.

"My brother was a good man," said Nelson, as if talking into the knife as a microphone. "But he thought he was something he wasn't. Thought he was a father. I was going to tell him the truth, that he wasn't no father to her, that it was you. But I didn't because I don't do that. Enough suffering in this world, that's why I spread holy joy.

"Sure am glad you came here to talk to me tonight, though. Wife's gone with my boy. Shit, maybe he's your kid, too. Holy Jesus knows I ain't been doing much fucking. Kid crawls around, grabbing at my stump, cries but not so loud that I can't sleep. Going to be just fine."

Jervis stood back while Nelson rambled away. He should be slicing him up, making it so Nelson couldn't talk, but his words were bouncing around his insides so much that he wasn't sure he wanted them to stop. He wanted to listen, felt like pacing, felt like hearing someone talk.

"You know why I'm here?" Jervis asked.

"Hell. Don't know for sure. Get visits all the time from the likes of you. Whatever the reason, only one thing I know for sure is, you're here because you're like me. Same God that made you, made me."

"Lilly, my girl," Jervis said. "You slammed her veins. Blew her out."

"I did her a favor. You think she'd have any moments worth living in her life without me? No fucking sir, would not. Same's you. You got dope in you and it's all you got out of this life. Now look at you. Your damn head looks like you tried to cut it off. At least they finished the job with my leg. You can't even finish it right, you stupid fuck."

"Yeah, well, I'm a dad now. Lilly's poppa. You don't know nothing about that. Your kid, he's going to be like me. Tortured by his own dad's voice forever. He'll curse you when you're dead."

"What do you know about being a dad?" Nelson said. "You been slamming her veins longer than me. You ain't ever gonna be that. You just like her other dad. Think you're something you're not."

"I know enough to know you'll be dead soon, but first I'm going to make you suffer. You're going to hate me before you die. You're going to regret what you did. You're going to remember my face even after you die."

Jervis felt his insides boiling. Red goosebumps were sticking out of his skin, his mouth was ready to breathe fire. He was ready to spill this man. Nelson didn't seem to care, but he would. Jervis would see to that.

"I've been visited by the likes of you a lot, right after I O.D. When I'm out cold they come to me. Much worse than you, my friend. Overdosed half a dozen times, that's the only time I get scared. When things crawl out of my insides to speak to me. My own kid clawing his eyes out and then licking his fingertips, my wife laughing at me while I swing on the gallows. That's why I got a wife. She grabs some Narcan and shoots it into me, makes the heroin and demons go right away."

"You got any dope?"

"Fuck yeah. Holding. Always holding in my orange duffle bag." Nelson nodded his head towards the bag on the coffee table. "That's the difference between you and me. I'm no desperate dope fiend, I'm on top of my shit."

Jervis grabbed the orange duffle bag. He rummaged through it while holding the knife at Nelson as if it were a pistol. Inside, he found fresh syringes and at least ten bags of dope. A supply. Nelson was different, not like addicts who need to scrap some metal or turn in some cans to get a ten dollar baggy of dope.

Next to the syringes were needles in a plastic package. They were fresh, like from a hospital, with plastic on the tips, like nothing he had ever seen.

"What the hell are these?"

"Narcan. Promised her I'd keep it with my dope. Bag always has ten or twenty of them."

"They get you high?"

"Au contraire, you asshole. I told you. You want to save someone from an overdose, you grab that. It sucks the dope right out of you, brings you back. You see the dark light, feel the cold, then it sucks you back to the warm. It's like getting born all over only you're born back into a sick fuck like me, not a baby."

"We ain't fucking friends, you got it?" Jervis said loud enough that dust shook from the lampshade. "I'll show you. If you got any veins left. I'll mix up half of this heroin, and your head will explode."

"Blow me up. Blow me straight the fuck up. I ain't scared of dying, I'm scared of not being able to get high anymore."

The man showed no fear, and it made the itch in Jervis's neck burn. He needed Nelson to pay for his crimes. He'd put him back in the terror of an overdose. The place where the demons visited. Where he saw images of his family tearing out his eyeballs or making him swing on the noose.

Jervis mixed up five baggies of dope, fixing it up like old times, like in Momma's basement. Five bags of dope in the syringe. If Nelson tried to run off, he'd cut him up, but Nelson couldn't run off with one leg. This was an execution, with Nelson tied to the chair.

When he slammed the twenty-five gauge needle into his jugular, Nelson's skin seemed thick as Lilly's black hide.

It didn't take long. His skin changed colors like a TV changing stations. His body spasmed like he was in an electric chair. Just before it seemed his head would burst, the spasms stopped and his head hung slack. Foam bubbled from his mouth. Jervis slapped him about with the back of his hand, whap, whap, on both cheeks. His head moved, but he did not wake. His eyelids were open a crack, and Jervis could see the white slit of his pupil like the sliver of the moon.

The demons of an overdose were visiting.

Jervis grabbed the man's one leg and tugged. Nelson slid from the chair to the floor without much effort. With the orange duffle bag over his shoulder, he pulled the weight of the man out the front door. It would be easy to drag him across the street like this.

I fetched him for you Lilly. I fetched him like you asked and I'm bringing him home.

CHAPTER SIX:
LILLY WITH CRYSTAL

HER SKIN WAS WARM, AND I CLUNG TO IT, wishing I could crawl right inside of her. Walking around the neighborhood with my nails dug into her back was like walking on the moon. Her holding onto me was all that stopped me from floating off into space. She was my lifeline for that moment. I felt the thud of each one of her heartbeats. We were walking the same path I had taken every day to my bus stop.

Except I had been alone every time I walked to school. This time I wasn't.

We walked by the twins' house, Ciara and Ciana's, in the dark of night. I could still see that their grass was mowed, for it didn't tower high like a field of wheat. Garbage cans were lined up neatly at the side of the house, like two gnomes standing guard. Their mom's Oldsmobile was parked in the driveway. A porch light was on and shined bright, and Oscar's mom held me tight as we walked on by.

She was just as sweet as Oscar said she was. Oscar talked a lot to me in my dark sleeps. Sometimes I would listen, sometimes not, but no matter what he'd still whisper to me about fire and smoke and books and his mother.

I pretended for a moment that the fires never happened. That Oscar didn't die in his own fire and that I never had my insides blow out the night of mine. That instead it was just a cool September morning and I was going to the bus stop with an empty belly, hoping I wasn't late and had time for a school breakfast of Cheerios.

Many houses down, the last working streetlight flickered like a jack-o-lantern candle. Soon enough, the light would die too, and stay dead. Stuck in this purgatory with me. So many houses blackened by flames around here. They stuck out like jagged pieces of black, broken teeth, and we walked by all of them.

Oscar's mom started to slow. I could feel my weight dragging her down. My belly started to churn, cells spinning inside ready to attack, to hurt me some more.

Where's Poppa Jervis? I need to get back. He'll be home soon, and if I am gone, something bad will happen.

"My eyes are closing, the dreams are coming, take me back," I told her.

But she doesn't take me back, I could tell by how her feet were moving. If I could have, I would've said it again. *Bring me back home. Put me in the basement with the rest of the dead bodies.* I felt her legs step up a front porch that wasn't mine. She knocked at the door, and soon enough someone inside unlocked the dead bolts. I couldn't open my eyes to see, but I heard a man's voice shout out, "What the hell is that? You alone? Anyone else here?" The door closed fast and was bolted behind us, then bolted twice more.

"It's just me, and hold on, just hold on for once, okay? Stop thinking everyone's looking to rob your dope."

"You're trying to steal it, for the fuck I know. And what is that? *Who* is that?"

"You know the girl. The one who they couldn't find."

I felt the man's brain start spinning while the oilfield in my head was being set on fire.

"That's who this is? Oh my fuck. Go dump that shit. Dump it in the back forty somewhere or in the field by Owl's."

"Owl's, huh? Owl's field is where Oscar kept walking out to play at night, and part of the reason I locked his door, and you just want to dump her there. Plus, this girl ain't a body, this girl is alive."

"Then put her on the road and see if an ambulance comes."

"It's not like that."

Another pause, and I felt eyes all over me. My ears clouded. Sounds faded.

"If that, if that *thing* is Zach Golson's girl, she doesn't have no right to be alive. By all rights, she should be dead. And you bring her here? Damn Crystal, have you lost your fucking mind?"

"I'm the only one around here who has a mind."

"Well, I might just happen to fire off my nine millimeter into her, don't care if she's a kid. Got Oscar's blood on her hands, and I'm not having it."

That's the last I heard until all sound faded. Tiny dark blood cells, the sharp ones, the ones that retreat when the dope is in my body, they returned and filled me up. My spine grew into a razor, cutting me down the middle.

I wanted to cry and let the pain drip free but couldn't open my eyes to shed the tears. I lay still, stuck in this dark, stuck on this street, stuck in this body. A black fly in a web, waiting for the voices and noises to come.

And they always do—noises that have been stuck in my memory come forth. The crushing noise of my dad's head from the metal pipe that Poppa Jervis smashed him with. It echoes in a place far off, and then I hear the splash when he falls into the bathtub where my Grandma floats, dead in her own tub full of blood. Then I see Mom's skull bobbing in the water, the grey flakes of her bone making tiny specks in the potion.

It was this potion that I injected into my veins, making me what I am.

The noises moosh into a soup being swirled in a cauldron and heated over a fire, but finally my mother's words bust out loud and clear.

THEY HATE YOU IN THAT HOUSE, LILLY. THEY HATED ME, AND THEY'LL HATE YOU.

When I hear it, I see it coming from her skull in the bathwater.

LILLY. YOU NEED TO COME WITH US. WE ARE HERE. WAITING. YOU SHOULD BE HERE WITH ME. I AM YOUR MOTHER. NOBODY ELSE CAN BE THAT FOR YOU.

The voice came from the thick blackness I was swimming in, a place with no floor, no direction, no gravity, the bottom of some ocean. The only signs of life were the tiny piranha with razor teeth, chewing at my insides. I didn't answer the voices. I never did. I knew I couldn't. That would change things. It would suck me down with them forever and I'd never get out. Instead, I just stayed quiet and waited for the prick of the needle from Poppa Jervis to wake me.

My grandmother's voice came next. It felt so close to my ear I could feel her wrinkled lips moving. *SHE DONE TRIED TO DIE, YOU KNOW SHE HAS. LILLY IS THE REAL WITCH, NOT ME. SHE'S A DEADLESS GIRL, THAT'S WHAT SHE IS. WHEN MY HEART STOPPED BEATING ONCE FOR LONG ENOUGH, I WAS DEAD FOR GOOD. BUT NOT LILLY, HER LIFE IS STRONGER THAN THAT.*

I done tried to die. My grandmother was right. In the basement across the street, I tried to cut myself up and make whatever was keeping me alive squeeze out. I wanted to bleed to death. But my skin is like blackened steak, and I couldn't cut it enough. Sometimes I just hoped something would stab through me. Sometimes I imagined burning myself up until I was tiny ashes, but I worried each piece would stay alive and I'd feel the burn forever.

LILLY? LILLY? It was Oscar calling out my name this time. His voice was the rainbow that popped up in the billowing black clouds of storms and electric shocks. It had color, youth, but I knew it wouldn't last. I knew I still couldn't answer. **LILLY. MY MOM WENT AND GOT YOU. SHE KNOWS HOW TO LOVE, SHE DOES, BUT YOU NEED TO GET OUT OF THERE. YOUR MOM'S RIGHT. AVANTI DOES HATE YOU. HE WILL HATE YOU. I KNOW THAT MAN. I SEEN HIM DO SOME TERRIBLE THINGS.**

I kept swimming in the cold dark black, sinking deeper, but waiting for Poppa Jervis. I needed the tiny prick with dope inside to stop the pain, to stop the voices. I hated to wait, and each time screamed for help on the inside, not with noises, but tears that had no eyes to drip from.

SOME DAY THEY'LL FORGET ABOUT YOU. THEY WILL LEAVE YOU ALL ALONE. POPPA JERVIS WILL BE GONE. NOBODY WILL BE THERE TO SAVE YOU. NOBODY TO GET YOU DOPE. NOBODY TO GET YOU MILK-BLOOD. THEN THEY'LL FIND YOUR BODY, BURY YOU IN A GRAVE, AND YOU'LL STAY LIKE THIS UNDER THE EARTH FOREVER. THAT'S WHY YOU SHOULD COME WITH US, LILLY.

YOU SHOULD COME WITH US, Oscar agreed.

I want to die, but I can't. I can't.

CHAPTER SEVEN:
JERVIS DRAGS UNCLE NELSON ACROSS THE STREET

"LILLY. LILLY! I'M HOME AND I GOT HIM. I got him. Got Nelson. Fetched him, just like you asked me."
Jervis plopped the bag full of heroin, syringes, and Narcan on the table like a sack of groceries long waited for. He dumped Nelson next to the fat man lying in the lake of blood. The place is a damn mess. Another body he had to get rid of before it got to smelling. But the fat man had milk-blood fresh still, and Lilly needed to be fed.

But first she needed to see her Uncle Nelson face to face.

The sun was near rising, and tiny bits of the thick dust swirling in the air started to show in beams of light. Lilly and him could get their morning fix together, sit in silence, let the memories of their life be gone, and instead enjoy a perfect day.

Lilly had to be in her sleep by now, waiting for him to wake her with some new blood. Or maybe he could boil up one of Nelson's packs of dope and shoot it into her. He needed to be a good dad, show Nelson what a good dad does. Prove that he knew how to love a daughter.

He stepped into the doorway of the back bedroom, expecting to see Lilly lying there in her sleep, but all he saw was the ashen mattress. Nothing. He reached down and scattered his hand back and forth. Objects like crumbs were brushed off the bed. There was no Lilly

The itch in his neck burned sharp and deep. He needed relief, but had no knife in his hand, no syringe in his pocket. Things felt empty.

She was in the basement. That was it. Basements were her favorite now. That's where she felt safe. He shouted out her name and moved his legs fast as the sound traveled, bounding down the stairs to get to her.

Bottom of the stairs, and his eyes adjusted to the dark. The basement needed cleaning. Bodies been piling up, some stinking, and there was no sign of Lilly in her usual spot. She liked to sit on the floor in a ball with her legs folded up into her arms, right next to the furnace. Eyes closed, waiting for him.

Jervis sifted through the bodies, limbs cold and stiff, faces he remembered from days past, most of them bone dry from blood, all of them still screaming in glass-shattering pain.

No Lilly. What to do?

"5486," he mumbled. "5486."

He paced in the basement. His hands checked his pockets for his food stamp card. Empty. Long ago empty. That card has been gone for weeks.

5486. He hadn't mumbled that code to himself in so long, hadn't wanted to. But now he needed it. It felt good to repeat it again and again and stop his brain from screeching thoughts of pain. *5486. Or was it 3486?*

Oh no. He needed Lilly. She was sleeping somewhere, feeling the pain, hearing the voices of dead ones. She needed her Poppa to wake her. He'd find her. She must be in a corner of this house somewhere, lying underneath a floorboard, drifting in a shadow. He'd find her and be a dad again.

He bounded up the stairs. Searched in corners, under furniture, inside the oven. Peeked at the front porch. Nothing. He grabbed his knife, twirled the tip into the gash of his neck, leaning his head into it like a dog being scratched, and groaned aloud.

Lilly. Gone? No. She can't be. I fetched Nelson for her.

Nelson. He looked down at the body. The man's mouth was foaming. A nerve in his cheek twitched. His energy was fading, and soon he would die. He looked like an overdose body you'd dump off at a hospital to die.

Jervis always thought he'd die looking like that. He'd been taken to so many hospitals looking just as sick. He'd woken up after flat-lining with doctors in white suits standing over him. Or he'd get caught talking to himself in a soup kitchen somewhere, screaming at the voices in his head, and someone would scoop him up and make him go to the hospital. The people there would ask him questions, trying to get into his brain. "Is there mental illness in your family? What medications do you take? Is there an emergency contact we can call? Do you have thoughts of hurting yourself?" He mumbled words to keep them happy, and soon enough he'd be in a hospital bed eating apple sauce out of a carton with a plastic spoon.

Then he'd see cockroaches running up and down their white, clean walls that nobody else could see.

No matter what he said they'd keep him there a few days, but it wasn't so bad. Fresh bedding. Pillows. Long showers where he'd watch the debris of the street wash off his body and circle down the drain. He'd sit in their therapy groups while his dad's voice whispered in his ear. *DON'T TELL THEM NOTHING. DON'T SAY NOTHING, JERVIS. IF YOU DO THEY WILL KNOW. THEY WILL KNOW YOU'RE A RED DEVIL.*

He knew how to put on a face to make them think his brain wasn't screaming in his skull, that his dad wasn't telling him how to kill, that the medications were working and he wouldn't kill himself.

Then they'd let him leave the hospital with a clean body and a belly full of food.

Nelson wasn't going to be taken to any hospital. He was going to get hurt, and hurt real bad. Whatever demons had crawled out of his spine and tormented him weren't enough. Nelson needed to pay for his crime.

Jervis shuffled through the duffel bag of dope, and pulled out the Narcan wrapped in its little plastic package. He split the plastic between his teeth, pulled the safety cap off, and then aimed it at the yellow body below him. *How the hell do you work this fucking thing?*

Who the fuck cares. He stabbed the needle into Nelson, hoping it would hurt. "Bam, there you go." He twisted the syringe inside, and if this didn't work, there were more in the bag to poke into Nelson's eyes.

But no more was needed, for within a few moments, Nelson's eyelids were fluttering. Foam bubbled from his mouth and he coughed, spastic, his body rolling to and fro. Jervis gave him a punt with his boot, right into his gut. *Umph*, the man's air shot out of his lungs and he sucked in more.

"You like that motherfucker?" Jervis yelled at him. "You want another?"

Jervis kicked again, and the impact opened Nelson's eyes all the way. He looked up at Jervis as if waking from the dead and unsure if he wanted to. He spoke through frothy lips.

"You stupid fuck," Nelson said. "A dad, huh? Well, the girl you call your daughter? I seen her. I seen Lilly. She's gone, isn't she? She's gone. I know it."

"The fuck you know anything."

"She is gone, isn't she?" he said, laughing. "She done left you. You went and got me, and she left, and now you're alone."

"Shut up. Shut up."

"I seen her where I was. I seen your dad, too. He wants to say a few words to you. Wants me to tell you some things. Says he's gonna talk to you. He says you should cut your whole damn head off."

Jervis paced away from the man. Looking at Nelson's face made his stomach burn, his neck itch.

5486, 5486.

"What's a good poppa like you gonna do now? You're really fucked."

Nelson's mouth full of foam was wrinkled into a smile. With his one leg cut off, he squirmed on the ground like a snake with arms. Jervis gave him another boot smack in the jaw, and Nelson's teeth smashed together. He fell flat on the ground, wiped the gunk and blood off his mouth with the back of his hand, and spit out some teeth.

"You know what's next?" Jervis screamed at him. "You know what a dad does when someone talks shit about his daughter? He sews their mouth shut. That's what I'm gonna do. Stick some needles into your fat lips, from top to bottom, maybe pinch your nose once in a while, then let go, then pinch, then let go, then you try to talk."

"Fine with me," said Nelson, his words making the bloody foam on his mouth bubble. "Know what else you can do? Just keep feeding me dope. I'll take the smack, I'll be your little bitch instead of her."

Knife or the pipe? Which one will shut him up?

Jervis needed the knife for his itch, so he grabbed the pipe and started raining two-handed blows on Nelson's face. The cold metal felt good in his hands. The noise of each impact softened his pain. He kept going until Nelson's face was mangled up nice and good, as good a job as he ever did before. When his work was done, sadness dripped, for Lilly hadn't a chance to see this. He had fetched him for her, it showed he loved her, that he was loyal. Now Nelson was crumpled on the ground with a purple face of moosh.

But the words kept coming.

JERVIS? JERVIS?

The words floated in the air like ash over a bonfire.

THAT DON'T MATTER, JERVIS. YOU RED DEVIL. THAT DON'T MATTER. YOU CAN BUST UP MY FACE, YOU CAN SEW MY LIPS TOGETHER. BUT YOU CAN'T CUT ME OUT OF YOUR INSIDES. I'M THERE FOREVER.

Jervis dropped the pipe. It clanked on the floor. Words kept coming from a voice he hadn't heard since before Lilly was in the fire.

YOU A DEVIL.

His dad's voice was back. Gone from his head so long, but now burrowing back in. Like the top of his own skull had split open, and the voices rushed in.

JERVIS. I HAVE ALWAYS BEEN HERE. YOU HAVEN'T BEEN RIGHT. I'M HERE TO MAKE YOU RIGHT AGAIN.

Jervis paced away from the body and touched his pant pockets searching for his card. He needed to leave, he needed his disability money. Where was his card? What was the pin number? 3476? 5486? He repeated the numbers hoping they'd come to him. They did not. His boots scuffled the ground.

JERVIS. IT'S OKAY. IT'S JUST ME AND YOU AGAIN. YOU'RE A RED DEVIL AND SHE'S A RED DEMON. LET ME TEACH YOU HOW TO BE A DAD. YOU AND I, SON. WE'LL TAKE CARE OF THINGS. I'M GOING TO TEACH YOU HOW TO BE HER DADDY.

CHAPTER EIGHT:
BACK TO CRYSTAL AND LILLY

"ZACHARY GOLSON'S DAUGHTER. You're letting her stay here. Here? In this house? My house? I ain't hearing that. If she's staying here, we need to make her suffer, like her dad did to Oscar."

"She's just staying in the basement."

"Yeah, well I just might be sending some of the nastiest crackhead freaks down there, too. You know the ones. They might like that there's a girl down there. Let's see what happens then?"

Crystal looked away, smoked a cigarette, and said nothing.

She stayed silent enough that he knew the conversation was over and went back to his cave. She watched him grab the Xbox controller and lay his 9 millimeter at his side, tapping on it with his fingertip, like he does, as if she's supposed to be scared. He shot her a gaze of disgust, and then put the wireless headphones on.

Now wasn't the time to push any argument. Avanti's friend owned a lawn maintenance company, and was going to cut her a check as if he was her employer. Few more days and she'd be back in Hastings's office, and she could say she was employed as a landscaper. Then the hobgoblin would find something else to bust her ass about.

She went to her room, dug into the closet, and got out the old handbag—it indeed was a handbag and not a purse—gaudy and large enough to stick your head inside. A smaller purse was inside the big purse. She loved the sound of unzipping them both and looking into her own private stash.

There were nearly fifty packs of dope inside, taken two or three at a time, completely unnoticed by Avanti. She skimmed them when he was weighing, or snuck into his supply while he blasted a rock or drank some Gilbey's gin. The roll of cash was nearly a thousand dollars now, mostly in twenties. Lesser bills she didn't bother with, but she kept the hundreds, fifties, and twenties. She'd been selling some on her own, sometimes pocketing bills, or overcharging idiot customers when Avanti wasn't around. Even though the cash was from the grubby hands of addicts all over this street, it warmed her soul to feel them against her fingertips. It was her ticket to escape this city. Money gotten by the most diseased minds and suffocating in this bag, but someday she'd tap into it and set herself free. She'd make a run to California and would have her own for once.

Deep in this same closet, she still kept some of Oscar's clothes. Most were damaged by the fire, but his drawer full of sleepover clothes at Gramma's house survived. She grabbed a blue shirt with Transformers on it—nothing most girls would wear, but as fresh as any—and some jean shorts she could belt up.

Their basement was damp and gross. It was the world where Avanti really did send crackheads who needed to smoke on the spot, and their paranoia could be felt hanging in the air. The sound of dripping water from some unknown source never left. Remains of forty ounce bottles and lighters that no longer worked lay nearby a pile of dirty laundry on the ground. An empty plastic bottle of detergent sat on the dryer. In the corners, spiders that only live in a basement such as this, who see in the dark, who know everything, spun their webs to capture and feed off the lesser creatures.

Lilly was lying down there on an old futon. A plug-in nightlight glowed on the wall and kept things from going full dark. Every few minutes, Crystal heard voices coming from the basement, and was sure Lilly had risen. She'd walk down and stand over her, but the girl was still sleeping. The only thing moving was Lilly's pupil fast and furious under her eyelid. Crystal tried to shake her awake by nudging her shoulder, softly at first, but then so much her whole body shook side to side. She called out her name, put a hand against her charred cheek, but nothing made those eyes open.

Crystal lit up a cigarette, sucked the smoke deep into her lungs, and then pushed the warm smoke down through each nostril towards her lips in a brilliant exhale. She remembered when she had tried to stop smoking; having a baby was going to change things. She was growing a purpose in her womb, a fragile being who needed her. A chance to live again. She could still see the sweet face of the baby boy. A younger, more promising version of herself.

But she wasn't able to keep the child safe. Oscar was destroyed, and so was she.

And now before her lay a child who said she was broken. She said there was only one way to wake her up. The needle. The one with the blood inside. It was capped and tucked in her dresser upstairs.

What harm would it do to inject her? This was the plan all along, wasn't it?

Crystal pounded her feet back up the stairs to retrieve the needle full of blood, and was panting when she came back down. She waited for her breath to steady. She held the needle in one hand, and held onto Lilly's hand with the other. Lilly's fingers, the round knuckles, so tiny, like an infant's in an incubator. The body seemed like some ancient fossilized person from an Egyptian tomb. The fact that she was lying here, on her basement futon, changed the laws of this street. Children killed on this street don't go to the place most souls go when they die.

Crystal's fingers trembled with the syringe in her hand, but she'd seen this done a thousand times before. When the needle pricked the rough, blackened armor of Lilly's skin, Crystal felt a shock in her own spine, like something had pricked her just as sharp. It went up the vertcbrae in her back, one by one, until it prickled the hair on her head and then rose right out of her. The child's arm was being flooded with this blood. She feared she was hurting her— but then again, a child like this could be hurt no more.

The plunger was pushed all the way in, and the syringe was emptied. Crystal lit up a cigarette and waited for Lilly to show some sign of life. It didn't take long. A bend in one knee, and then the other. Both legs were balled up against her. Her arm moved and she rubbed her fingertips across her forehead.

And then her eyes opened.

Crystal felt she had just oiled the Tin Man.

Lilly's eyelashes fluttered and her hazy eyes looked around the room. The poor girl had woken in some strange basement, but that didn't stop her lips from curling into a heart-warming smile.

"Good morning," Crystal said. She imagined for a moment she was waking her own daughter up for school, making her breakfast, packing her lunch—but she'd lost the chance for such a life long ago.

Lilly picked up the empty syringe and held it in her hand.

"That's what I used. I did what you said, I used it to wake you up."

"Thank you."

Lilly sat up on the futon with her feet touching the cold cement of the basement floor. The lone light cast shadows on the spiders and shards of broken crack pipes in the corner. Lilly looked into each of them.

"I don't know what you are," Crystal said in a hushed voice, "but I know that there's something true about you that I won't find anywhere else. There's lots I want to know from you. Like when you say *ashes talk to ashes,* that means Oscar's here on this street, like I thought. That means I'm right?"

Crystal wished she had waited a bit longer to start asking these things, but she'd waited long enough in prison and could wait no more. In order to slow herself down, she inhaled from her cigarette, blew it out the side of her mouth, and rolled it between her fingers. The paler skin on the undersides of her fingertips had yellowed from the constant twiddling of nicotine sticks. Lilly had certainly noticed.

"I know, I smoke too much. But you might be someone who understands why."

"Why?" Lilly asked.

"You want to know why?"

"No, why would I understand?"

"Because you know how smoke, how fire–" she said, puffing her cigarette. "You know how it changes things."

"Like Oscar," she said.

Crystal put a hand on the girl's shoulder, felt her flinch for a second, and then relax.

"There's not a moment that goes by where I don't think of him. In his bedroom, trapped, screaming for me to help him. I see the house in flames, starting with the front curtains when the firebomb crashed through the window. The paneling burning, the couch, the roof, the firemen coming so long afterwards like they do in these parts.

"They told me he didn't die from the flames. They said it was the smoke. It filled his lungs, he couldn't get out. I sat in prison for years wondering about his last thoughts. What did it feel like? How much did it hurt? Did he feel loved? Did he feel the depths that he was loved, just for who he is? He was the only part of me I loved and I tried too hard, too hard to keep him safe. I tried to stop him from sneaking out at night like he did sometimes, having the police bringing him home when he snuck out to Owl's for an icee or to look at the stars, thinking he could see them with dollar store binoculars.

"Plus there were things going on in our house that he shouldn't see. I needed to keep him from walking out of his room on certain nights.

"But it killed him. Gross negligence, they called it."

Gross negligence. Just saying those words made Crystal's chest thump as if she was about to be sentenced to prison again.

"So I smoke a lot, and I smoke deep, because I want to feel like he did at that moment when he died from smoke in his lungs. Every day I am alive, I want to feel what he felt the day he died. I want it to scald my insides. To burn my lungs. I'm going to smoke until I can't breathe, trying to be him, I guess."

Lilly's white eyes sparkled, just a touch. A glimpse into something inside of her darkened body that was more glorious.

"Seemed right that I was trapped, locked in prison, like Oscar was. Wasn't right that I was alive and he was dead. Many times I wanted a prison fire. Wanted it to burn. Even though I'm out, I'm still not free, just walking around in a bigger cage."

Lilly laid back down, and Crystal felt the girl's energy fading and her muscles tightening. "I need another shot," Lilly said. "One just wakes me up, two keeps me going."

"I got some upstairs, of course."

"Straight heroin feels better," Lilly said without apology. "It's what I like. No memory residue like comes with the milk-blood of others."

"Stay here. I'll be back. But after I fix you up with some more, I want you to tell me what you know. You said you talk to Oscar. I want you to tell me. What was he thinking just before he died?"

The question hung in the damp basement as Crystal ascended up the stairs. No footsteps upstairs meant Avanti was still in his room, and there were no customers. She'd be able to go unnoticed and grab some nice Fentanyl-laced dope that would smack Lilly into the most powerful child this street had ever seen. Avanti wouldn't know what happened.

With each step she took, Crystal realized she was needed again. Someone was waiting on her. It'd been so long, and this time she would keep her child safe.

When she opened the basement door at the top, she started to worry—what if Lilly doesn't want to stay here? What if she sneaks out? Should she keep the girl down there for her own good? If she were to leave, it could mean a new kind of hurt she could stumble upon.

Crystal looked at the door jamb and remembered drilling the lock on Oscar's bedroom door after he'd wandered off more than once, the final straw being when he stepped out of his room at two in the morning and saw dope men shooting up in his living room.

She was trying to protect Oscar from these things. That was love, wasn't it?

No, if you really had love, you wouldn't let dope inside your house at all.

These thoughts didn't always get into her skull. She'd learned how to excuse herself, knowing that her reality wasn't like the rest of the world's. You couldn't do the right thing around here. The streets soaked inside your body, layer by layer, until it changed your soul. No amount of good intents or armor of defenses could keep that out.

But after seeing Lilly's soft eyes open, Crystal knew the girl's soul hadn't been fully burnt. It was there and it was safe. Like a new mom going to the fridge to prepare a bottle, she would get the girl the heroin she needed.

A knock on the door stopped everything. Somebody was there. Another knock followed. This one was fast and powerful with meaty knuckles, and Crystal felt something ripple inside her. She pulled aside the window shade to see the police car parked curbside out front. No policeman inside.

He was at the front door.

Crystal clenched her fists, digging her nails into her palm. There were steps to take. What to do? They had plans if the house was about to be raided—had even practiced them—but never with a body in the basement. This was not a 'no-knock raid,' that was for sure.

It's Agent Hastings. She figured out I'm living here, and as soon as the door opens I'll hear the words: "We're here to see the body in the basement."

Crystal peered around the corner, and immediately felt relief.

It was Officer Stinson.

Stinson: a round bellied, grey-bearded, cop they knew plenty well, who had no plans of busting them. Stinson had told Avanti many times, "I know you're selling, there's going to be somebody selling on this street for sure, but nobody needs to be staying here to get high. Sell to them and move them out."

A couple times, Stinson had bought some weed from them himself. More often, it was women he wanted. Last month he wanted three women to deal blackjack at a bachelor party, and other party favors if the money was right. Avanti hooked him up with these things, pretended to be buds with Stinson, while Stinson pretended to be a real cop.

Stinson could still go full-cop and try to be a hero any minute, and Crystal had no plans of talking to him. She walked to the room where Avanti was flat out in bed. His instinct was fading, because he had no idea who was at the door. He finally saw her body language, pulled off the headphones, and she had his attention.

"Stinson. He's at the door."

He got up to deal with it, and she went to the closet to rummage through her stash. Crystal heard Avanti and Stinson talking while she thumbed through the dope and money.

"Listen. About why I'm here," she heard Stinson say. "You know anything about a white kid on this street who got his head busted up and leg broke real bad? Came here, I think, and then his friend come up missing."

"Nobody I know like that. Won't sell a thing to them if they come here already like that."

"Well, listen, it's not just him. There's been quite a few lately. You know anything about your neighbor Nelson Golson? I know he's been purchasing from here. Someone robbed his house and now we can't find him."

"Well, he ain't ever come here himself."

"You know, people come up missing, things change around here. You need to do more for me. You aren't getting everything for free."

"Well, maybe I can get you something you want."

"And what's that? You tell me what you think I want," Stinson asked with words that were drooling.

"I know you like a piece of ass. I got that. I got some weird shit. I know you cops do some freaky shit. Well, I got a girl for you right now. She's in the basement. You never had a girl like her before, I don't think. You want me to show you?"

Stinson paused and Crystal's heart thunder-clapped against her chest. She breathed through her nose, holding it in. No answer came. Avanti was waiting for an answer, certainly hoping Stinson would say yes, and then he'd have even more of the cop in his back-pocket.

The air in the closet grew hot, sweat immediately started beading on Crystal's back. Still no answer, just a few soft words mumbled. Crystal zipped the handbag up, stuffed it back deep in its spot, and put the dope in her pocket. She got on her tiptoes, ready to dash to the basement and stop this any way she could if it went down.

"Listen, that sounds good," Stinson said. "Something like that. You need to think like that. Keep thinking like that, and we'll talk later. But don't be letting people come up missing around here."

Stinson's last words remained in the air long after the door slammed, and Crystal couldn't get her heart to stop pumping. One thing was clear.

In order to keep Lilly safe, she was going to have to lock her in.

CHAPTER NINE:

BACK TO JERVIS WITH NELSON AND OTHER SURPRISES

UPSTAIRS WASN'T SAFE. A police car was parked across the street, and the cop was walking from house to house, knocking on doors, and talking to people on their porches. Times like these, Jervis knew to stay hidden, so he'd dragged the bodies downstairs. Now he was safe in the basement with some dead people who were no help.

His disability money comes the first of each month, and he was searching his brain for the code to withdraw.

3476

5476

He paced from wall to wall, trying to pluck the digits from memory with each step. With the tip of his knife, he scratched the top of his head, right where he thought the memory was stuck, but still he couldn't remember the pin number from his disability account. Sirens screamed in his ears, and exploded out goosebumps in his skin. Tiny volcanoes were erupting everywhere.

If he could figure it out, he'd be okay. He'd have money again, dope, a place to stay, like old times. But the pacing didn't help. And the card? Where was his food stamp card? He patted his pockets front and back but nothing. He'd lost it.

No, that doesn't matter. None of that does. Remember you're a Poppa. The number doesn't matter. Where is Lilly? Just get her back here. That's what matters.

A sharp pain stung his neck, so he took the knife, twirled the tip on his itch, and paced. Two steps, turn, two steps, turn, and then the voice of his dad came back.

YOUR ITCH. IT NEVER GOES AWAY. YOU CAN SCRATCH AND DIG, CLAW AND CUT, BUT IT WILL BURN UNTIL YOU FINISH THE JOB AND LOB OFF YOUR HEAD ALL THE WAY. WE CAN FINISH THE JOB TOGETHER, MY SON.

Jervis grabbed the pipe, smashed it again against Nelson's face, and stood over him, waiting for the man to say another word. Nothing. He dropped the pipe and the clanking noise cut into his ears. The bodies on the ground mumbled their complaints. The darkness vibrated. Dust in the air scattered. The boom of his dad's voice kept getting louder.

JERVIS. IT'S JUST ME AND YOU AGAIN. ME AND MY RED DEVIL SON. THAT DAUGHTER OF YOURS, SHE'S A RED DEMON. YOU NEED SOMEONE LIKE ME. I'M GOING TO TEACH YOU HOW TO BE A DAD. YOU AND ME SON, WE'LL TAKE CARE OF THINGS.

Go upstairs. Quiet the voices. Leave them down here.
JERVIS. WE CAN BE A TEAM.

The voices kept coming, no matter how fast he paced, no matter what he tried to fill his brain with, he couldn't shut them up. He'd busted up Nelson's face to make sure he couldn't say anymore, and the fat dope fiend he'd just nabbed was twisted up into a blood-soaked pretzel. But still they came.

NOTHING YOU CAN DO. DID YOU FORGET I'M INSIDE OF YOU FOREVER?

You can't get me anymore, Dad. I won. I beat you. I took your ashes out of the jar. I boiled them in water. I filled the syringe and shot them in my vein. I used you. I needed to get high and used you and now I have all your days of dope inside me and more. I have a daughter and I'm going to find her and you are nothing.

YOU PUT ME INTO THE MEMBRANES OF YOUR SKULL, COATED YOUR INSIDES WITH ME. I'M PART OF YOU FOREVER.

It was in a dark basement like this that Jervis was heroin sick. How long ago was that? Was that really him? So sick, so suffering. Locked down there by his mom with only his dad's ashes for company. He shot his dad up, knowing that with all the heroin his dad had used over the years there must be something left in the ashes. What a rush it was when he got high from Dad's ashes. His insides had been blackened ever since.

SEE. YOU REMEMBER. NOW DO IT AGAIN. ONCE MORE. BUT THIS TIME WITH YOUR DAUGHTER. YOU REALLY LOVE HER? DO WHAT YOU DO BEST, CHOP HER UP IN LITTLE PIECES, SHOOT UP EACH BIT OF HER INTO YOUR SICK SELF. ALL OF HER. IT WILL FIX YOU RIGHT UP, YOU WON'T BE SICK NO MORE. MAKE HER PART OF YOU FOREVER.

I wouldn't do that to her. I'm all she has. The only one who loves her.

The image of what his dad described crept into his brain. Jervis couldn't stop it. He saw himself chopping her up, one tiny piece at a time. First he'd peel her skin right off, like a big sunburn, scraping the dry, charcoal pieces off and then boiling them in water. He could see himself sucking it all up in the tip of the syringe, and then plunging part of her inside of him. Ahhhhhhhh, with all that he's been injecting into her body, what kind of high could that be? Thinking about it made him shiver. And she'd be alive, and could watch it all, and be part of her daddy forever.

SHE WOULD BE PART OF US FOREVER.

That's not what I want. I want to find her and bring her back home and live like Dad and daughter again. Provide for her, make her happy. She needs me.

YOU'RE A RED DEVIL AND SHE'S A RED DEMON AND NEEDS YOU TO INJECT HER INTO YOUR VEINS PIECE BY PIECE, ONE SQUISHY EYEBALL THEN THE NEXT, OH WHAT A GLORIOUS TIME WE WILL HAVE.

No, I am her Poppa. I'm not like you. You beat Mom so hard I can still hear the smacking noise.

YOU'RE SHOOTING UP YOUR OWN GODDAMN KID WITH HEROIN. YOU ARE WORSE THAN ANY FUCKING THING I EVER BEEN. YOU THINK A GOOD DAD WOULD LET THEIR CHILD WANDER OFF LIKE SHE DID? SHE'S NOT YOUR GIRL, YOU'RE HER BITCH NOW. YOU KNOW WHAT I WOULD HAVE DONE TO YOU IF YOU'D WANDERED OFF?

You'd not have known, not have cared.

Jervis tried not to think it, but Dad was right. Lilly didn't know how to take care of herself around here. She needed a father to teach her how. That's what dads do, they teach their kids how to survive, make sure they're fed, make sure they're safe. He needed to find her and somehow make her part of him forever.

No, that's not what good poppas do. It would hurt her, destroy her.

YES. DO IT, BIT BY BIT. LET HER WATCH. YOU'LL BE HER DAD FOREVER. FETCH HER, FETCH HER NOW.

Fetch her. Dad was right about that, he did need to fetch her and take care of her. Someone could be hurting her now, someone who didn't love her like he did.

Memories of the last few weeks came back to him. Watching over her as she was in her sleep, seeing her wake each day when he gave her the morning shot of milk-blood. The sweet smell of her ashen body, knowing that it was him who she needed. If he could find her he could have that all back.

Jervis. Another voice spoke to him. **Jervis. I know where she is. I can tell you.**

It was the voice of a woman. A voice he'd heard before. It seemed wet, frigid, like a drippy leak from a cold pipe.

You know me. You put her inside of me. I'm Lilly's mother. Lilly is with another woman. Someone who thinks she can take my place. I won't have that. You go to her house. Kill her. Do her like you do.

Where? Which one?

The house with the dope, you know the one. Her house has more dope than you will ever need.

It was time to go on a hunt for Lilly. Jervis grabbed the orange duffel bag, added the metal pipe and the long butcher knife, and he was ready. Ready to do battle and get his daughter back.

CHAPTER TEN:
LILLY IN THE BASEMENT

I WAS ALONE IN THE BASEMENT. All was dark, all was quiet. Once in a while tiny creaks whispered about the stranger among them, but soon enough they got used to me and went silent.

Oscar's mom left to get me more dope. I heard her footsteps tapping up the stairs, fast, confident, smooth, not like Poppa's boots that went bang, bang, bang everywhere and made earthquakes on the ground.

Where was Poppa? Gone to fetch Nelson, like I asked him to. When he came back, he'd find the house empty.

Now this woman had me in her house, but left me all alone. She'd be back soon. She was getting me more, she said she was. She would want to know about Oscar.

How could I tell her that Oscar sometimes acted like he didn't even die? That he just floated up out of his body with the smoke somewhere? That he was still waiting for her, really, in his room, in this street, in the air; the place where all smoke rises.

I needed her to come back down to the basement. Soon, my eyes would close and my world would go full dark again. The tiny razor chips that slice up my insides, that hide in the corners of my body, would come out to dig their claws into me.

Would this woman take care of me like Poppa Jervis did? Poppa knew how to take away my suffering. But even when he did, I would just sit with him and wonder how I could make my life end faster. I'd given up my dreams that anyone could make me regular again. I had become defective all over, not just in my heart.

The darkness started to cloud and the tiny creatures inside of me came forth. They were feeding on my spine with their sharp teeth, biting with fury in the blackness. And then came the faceless voices:

I TOLD YOU SHE WOULD LEAVE YOU. YOU'RE ALONE AND SOMEDAY IT WILL NOT JUST BE IN A BASEMENT BUT BURIED IN A GRAVE. STUCK IN A CASKET. OR MAYBE IN TINY ASHES, EACH ONE OF THEM IN PAIN. THAT WOMAN DOESN'T LOVE YOU. SHE'S JUST USING YOU. I AM THE ONE WHO WAS MURDERED BECAUSE OF YOU. I WON'T LET HER ACT LIKE SHE'S YOUR MOTHER. YOU KNOW THAT, RIGHT?

I pretended not to hear, but it was like she knew what I was scared of and kept pounding me over the head with it.

WHEN SHE GOES BACK TO HER MOM'S HOUSE, I WILL BE THERE. I WILL GET HER MOM. WHEN HER MOM BREATHES, I WILL BE IN THE AIR AND GET INTO HER HEAD. REMEMBER YOUR GRANDMOTHER?

I did remember the way she got into my grandmother, but I didn't answer. It felt like one word back and my soul would get sucked down into some place I didn't want to be.

Oscar started whispering to me with his warm voice. *LILLY. YOU'LL BE OKAY. MY MOM WILL BE GOOD TO YOU. SHE WILL. YOU'RE LUCKY, BUT YOU HAVE TO REMEMBER*... Oscar's words were destroyed mid-sentence when I felt a sharp prick in my arm. His mom was back, and her dope was strong, like nothing I'd had before. It made my defective heart fire, the pain receded in an instant, and I opened my eyes to see her looking over me. Her hair dangled along the sides of my head.

"Hey you. Sorry it took me a while. I got caught up. Someone was upstairs. You're safe here though. And I will do what I need to do to keep it that way. And look what I got." She opened the palm of her hand and showed tiny baggies of more heroin cupped inside, then closed her fist over them like a magician.

"Thank you," I said. "Why are you doing this?"

"You are the reason I am back on this street. You proved to me that I'm right to stay here. That there's more to learn. You say you hear Oscar. We need to talk about that. But first, I know you need more."

She presented another syringe, ready to go. Her warm fingers took my other arm and turned it to its underside. The needle pricked my skin, and there was such an electric jolt of warmth I shot my head up into the air. I felt like a cat, purring, each vertebrae of my spine coming alive. Warmness spread through my chest. Everything fluid and golden on the inside.

She waited, watched, didn't pressure me, but I could tell she wanted something in return. Upstairs, I heard shuffles, door locks and dead bolts being undone. Footsteps and voices. People coming in and out, and I was stuck down here knowing of them, but them not knowing of me.

"You know it was my dad, right? The man who raised me, you know it was him, right?"

"Yes, I know."

"You know he was the one who started the fire. He threw the firebomb onto your porch. That's what killed Oscar. Even if it wasn't the fire, but the smoke that killed him. You should hate me."

Crystal brushed a hand across my face, and it didn't feel like hate.

"It's not that simple. I know how it works on Brentwood. Your family hurts mine, and I hurt yours back. That's how it goes around here, and how it will go. None of us here been born to a normal life. We've been born in a dark basement of this world. Sometimes I think it was a sin to bring a new life onto this street.

"But your daddy—because he was your daddy, since he's the one that raised you—your daddy had something different in him. He probably killed half a dozen men on the block, but in the end, we all knew he was soft. And we knew it was your mom who was in his head, telling him we were disrespecting him. Whispering how he was being punked out by us. Your mom manipulated people to do things for her. I know that. Avanti knows that. She'd been doing it to Zach for years. She probably loved you like I loved Oscar, I'm not saying nothing against that, I just know she can get into people's heads and make them do things."

"She still can. She still can," I said, but Oscar's mom wasn't listening and just kept talking.

"Oscar's dad had better connections than Avanti will ever have. That maybe was a threat, but it was more than that. Your mom didn't like me. Didn't like the way others looked at me. Didn't like that I wasn't looking for attention the way she was, that I got it more. That's why it happened."

"What happened that night?" I asked.

"The night Oscar died you mean? It all started because we had to meet someone coming from Chicago with a ton of dope, meeting them halfway. I didn't want to go, but Oscar's dad isn't someone you say no to. He didn't trust anybody else to go.

"We left the house at ten. Oscar was sleeping, I made sure of that. The house was locked, and his room was padlocked so he couldn't leave. We'd be back by a couple hours after midnight, the latest. Four hours, Oscar would never know. All of this for a profit margin of twenty grand, so they said.

"Well, they were late, like dope-men always are, and we didn't get back until maybe five in the morning.

"We saw the fire trucks and police when we pulled down the street, and then we smelled the smoke. There was no fire anymore, just smoldering bits of our house and men in uniform out front walking about, nobody in much of a rush. Our hearts were thumping, both of us scared as hell that we'd been raided. I walked up, greeted by a cop who wouldn't tell me anything, wouldn't answer my questions, but instead started asking me a billion questions.

"'Was that your son in the house?' 'Was that him in the back room?' 'How long were you gone?' 'You locked it, right? You had a lock on it so he couldn't get out?' I answered fast, 'yes, yes, yes,' just to get him to answer me, to tell me where Oscar was.

"After he got me to incriminate myself, that's when he told me. Oscar was at Detroit Children's Hospital. That's where I could go to identify the body. Said he was sorry for my loss. I was charged three days later."

Her voice trailed off and she stopped her story. I wondered if Oscar could hear this. I listened for him, but nothing. Maybe he was sitting in silence like me.

"Lilly, I think you can answer the question that has been burning me up for years. What was he thinking those last moments before he died? What did he go through? Do you have any idea?"

"Yes, he told me some."

"Please, I need to know."

My head hurt to think of what to say and how to say it. I rubbed my fingers across my arm and felt the tiny track marks like I was some blind man reading braille. I thought of pausing, of asking for another shot of dope, or asking if I could just sleep for the night and talk tomorrow. But her eyes were open so wide, each of them glowing bright in this dark basement, every tiny bit of her waiting for what I had to say. So I told her.

"Here's what I know. I know he was sleeping and had no idea you were gone. He woke up when he heard the crash. Just thought somebody broke in. He tried to stay under his covers and hide. Then he waited and fell back asleep until the heat woke him up. He heard the crackle of the flames and knew it was a fire. He did try to get out, pulled on the door handle hard. But he'd done that before and knew it wouldn't open.

"He didn't scream. He never screamed. Don't worry about that.

"Firemen had visited his school. They visited mine, too. He remembered what they taught him to do in a fire, like stay close to the ground, stuff like that. That's what he did, he laid there on the ground next to the door. Lying there. Waiting. He closed his eyes and when he opened them again, the room was black with smoke. It swirled on the ceiling, billowed, spoke his name, and he wasn't scared anymore. He rose up with the smoke, and the only pain he felt was a big explosion in his chest. Next thing he knew he was up with the smoke, on the ceiling, where all smoke rises, and that didn't feel so bad. He wasn't scared—he knew you'd be back. He knows, don't worry, he knows."

Oscar's mom squeezed my hand. A stream of tears ran from her eyes, down to her chin. I watched it drip. The lies I told her weren't that big, and they were the kind I think a mom would want to hear.

"When you sleep, Lilly, when you're out like that, does it hurt bad?"

"Like my backbone is on fire and scorching everything around it. Yes."

"I'll take care of you. We'll figure out what to do, how to help you. But I need to know more. I need to feel like I'm with him. Like you're speaking with his voice, from where he is. If you do that, I'll make you feel good. Every day. We have a lot of dope here, more always comes, and Avanti isn't too sharp. I can help you."

I smiled big enough for her to see. People have been making promises to help me lots of times before. I knew not to expect it to happen, I knew to just smile and make them feel good that they were trying to help, even though I knew they'd try but fail.

"I have somewhere I have to go. I have to leave here tonight, but I'll be back tomorrow. I'll keep you safe. First you need to get cleaned up. A warm bath. Maybe something with your hair. I'll bring you upstairs when things settle down. When it's safe. When he's gone."

She left me there again. I listened to the sounds of feet shuffling upstairs and Avanti's voice getting loud, all enough to make dust fall from the wooden beams above. Later on, after the noises stopped, Oscar's mom held my hand and walked me up from the basement. The light upstairs was piercing. I couldn't see Avanti anywhere, but it felt like he was close by.

"Don't worry. He's gone. There's a bath for you."

The air in the bathroom was humid, the bathtub was full, and a folded dry towel was on the sink with fresh clothes. When Oscar's mom closed the door, I looked at the water, completely still and safe, but it seemed there might be sharks underneath the depths. A drop fell from the faucet, a tiny splash echoed, and then silence again. I wasn't sure I should get in, I wasn't sure I should be here. When I finally did go under the water, my skin tingled, like it was still red hot from the night of the fire and now being cooled. Like lava from a volcano hitting the ocean.

I went all the way under and my hair waved in the water like a little octopus swimming. I lay there adrift, letting the waves take me, pushing me this way and that, just like the people who were taking me places, and I had no choice but to go along. The mop of my hair grew under me. It got longer, started flowing. It slithered like a snake and wrapped around my neck, tried to get into my eyes, and pulled me down.

It wasn't even my hair anymore, and I knew whose hair it was:

LILLY. IT'S ME. I'M HERE. REMEMBER THIS? THIS IS HOW I DID YOUR GRANDMOTHER. YOU THINK YOU ARE SAFE IN HERE? I COME UP THROUGH THE CRACKS. I'VE DONE IT BEFORE, I WILL DO IT AGAIN. I KNOW HOW TO GET HER. I WILL. I WILL PUT HER BACK IN PRISON THROUGH THE TUNNELS AND TUBES OF THE UNDERGROUND. INTO THEIR AIRWAYS, INTO THEIR LUNGS. THE WOMAN IS LEAVING YOU SOON, AND YOU WILL NEVER SEE HER AGAIN. I KNOW HOW MUCH YOU HATE HOW YOU ARE, BUT YOU WILL ALWAYS BE THIS WAY.

My mom's voice stayed there even after the hair untangled from my body, and I knew what she said was true. I would never be regular again. I wouldn't risk hoping for something different.

Even though the bath towel was soft, it hurt my skin to dry off. I was a lizard that'd been roasted on a spit. I put on the blue t-shirt that was laid out for me. I knew it used to be Oscar's.

Oscar's mom waited for me outside the bathroom door and led me back downstairs. My time upstairs was enough—the basement was my place. She shot two more fresh packs of heroin into my arms, one on the left, one on the right, and then left me there, promising to be back after giving me a hug.

"I'm sorry to do this. I wish I didn't have to go," she said.

But she did go, and I stayed there with the glow of the nightlight to keep me company. I listened to the insects scurry in the basement, heard the time pass, and felt like I was close to the middle of the earth and could feel its heart beat. Once in a while I felt the stomp of feet upstairs, the front door opening, lots of voices, and then the door closing and getting bolted shut. I waited there, my eyes went dark, and my insides started to hurt again.

CHAPTER ELEVEN:
CRYSTAL GOES BACK TO HER PAROLE AGENT

IT WAS THE DAY BEFORE HER REPORT DATE. Crystal had to report to her parole officer, and if she got there at 10 a.m., shortly after the morning rush but before the lunch crowd, she could get in and out in less than two hours.

She drove off under the cover of darkness the night before to sleep at her mother's house. Lilly was locked in the basement, padlocked, and Avanti hadn't even noticed. Nor did Lilly, for she would soon be in her sleep, or wherever it was she went when the heroin faded, but it was easier that way. Crystal would bring her back as soon as she got home.

She had a payroll check from one of Avanti's customers. The man mowed lawns all day so he could make enough money to buy enough dope to fuel himself to mow lawns all day. The check made it look like she was employed in his landscaping company. She'd present it to Agent Hastings, who would scan it with her hobgoblin eyes. Soon enough, she'd find something else wrong that Crystal was doing and the fight would go on, but Crystal would not lose this round. Having this payroll check would make today's visit victorious.

She crept along, driving two miles under speed limit, so much on her mind with Oscar and Lilly and Stinson and fake payroll checks when she realized what she'd forgotten.

Her license plate. Shit. It was still in the kitchen from when she took it inside so it wouldn't get stolen. Being extra safe—always taking extra steps to keep things safe— but fucking up again. Here she was, driving without a license plate and worried about speed limits. A cop car anywhere behind her would notice. *I'm sorry officer, but I take off the license plate since our last one got stolen, and I can't risk having that happen again.* A cop wouldn't understand or believe that. She thought of turning back.

Instead, she went forward, telling herself how stupid she was with every moment that passed. She sucked down her cigarettes fast as she could, and only had six left. She hadn't brought any cash, and her gas gauge was at zero.

She was off her game.

She'd have to get ten bucks from her mom to fill up the tank on her way to Agent Hastings. Better yet, four bucks for gas, six for cigarettes.

She wished she could just dip into her whole stash of money and bring it with her, and then break for California if a parole visit went bad, but you don't walk out the front door on Brentwood with money in your pocket unless you're also carrying a gun.

With each moment she drove, all she could see in her mind's eye was the red and blue flashing lights of a cruiser pulling her over. Each car behind her creeping close was an unmarked car running her plates (she had no goddamn plates), who would then pull her over in moments, most definitely asking her to get out of the car. Then they'd take her back to Brentwood saying, 'We want to see the body in your basement.'

Why was she risking this for a dead girl? A girl who seemed dead at least, and a dope fiend like none other.

It's because of your dead boy.

The terror faded as she got closer and closer to the safety of her mom's house. Party stores selling forty ounce malt liquor, three for six bucks, gave way to real grocery stores. Closed down shops with broken signs and bars still on their windows gave way to active restaurants. She felt like a spy in enemy territory when she pulled down her mom's street.

Her mom's house was on a tree-lined street. It was a small ranch, white brick, a roof darkened by the brushing of branches over the years. A flag post waved in the front that her mother took great pains to change based on the season. Crystal backed into the driveway to disguise her current lack of a license plate. Shutting off the engine let her heart rest a bit. Air around there was fresh and easier to breathe. She stood outside the car for moments, waiting for the place to accept her. The dark of night always did, wherever she was.

Some of the neighbors might remember her from years ago, when Oscar and her would visit, but at this hour, they were dug deep into their homes. One light was on in her mother's house, but she was certainly asleep inside. Her mom drew the shades at 7:30 p.m. sharp, was asleep before nine, and woke at five. That's the schedule when you're old. Things slow, insides die, old dreams are forgotten.

Crystal opened the front door to the dim lights from the kitchen microwave, and another from the bathroom hallway. Mom's bedroom door was ajar and the hallway light spilled through the door crack. Crystal took a step inside. Her mom's breathing was heavy and more raspy than usual. Her jaw was slack and her mouth hung open, and the oxygen tank that she carried with her everywhere was bedside. Every inhale she took into her nostrils came from the metal canister through the plastic tubes.

Crystal went to the back porch and smoked consecutive cigarettes, blowing smoke into the air like a dragon, wondering what it was like back in the basement on Brentwood. Lilly was safe, and Crystal would make sure she stayed that way. Lilly was the closest thing to Oscar she'd ever hoped to find, and in fact, talked to Oscar, because *ashes talk to ashes*.

The bed in the spare room was made up hotel-style, and Crystal was wrapped tightly under the freshly washed sheets but slept little. She spent most of the night awake, waiting for the sun to rise. Before it did, she heard her mother get out of bed. The noise of her oxygen tank dragging behind her sounded like a shopping cart, and her rhythmic breaths from the tank made *phifffff – foooo, phifffff-foooooo* noises. Coffee cups clanked while her mother made tea with honey and heated water to make Crystal a cup of freeze-dried instant coffee.

It was time to get this day over. She pulled herself out of bed. Her mom was sitting in her chair under the soft light, tea steaming next to her.

"You haven't called me in days. You haven't been home like you said. You haven't been sleeping."

Crystal leaned down to give her mom a hug so she didn't have to move, then poured hot water into the coffee cup already filled with instant mix. She brought the cup to her lips, but the water scalded her tongue. The first sip would have to wait. She sat down on the couch without a word.

"I could feel you here, Cristi, lying in bed last night, not sleeping. Always known when you weren't sleeping."

"That's okay, I like to sit in bed and think. How's your hip?"

"Getting around better than you." She sipped her tea to add an exclamation point.

"Nobody came by here, right?" Crystal asked, as she always did to see if Hastings paid one of her home visits.

"Not the person you're thinking of. Just some man selling cable. Listened to him, is all I did."

Next to Mom's teacup was the massive supply of her monthly medications, arranged in daily doses in a plastic dispenser. Glucosamine, Lisinopril, Neurontin, Lipitor, Cymbalta, Vicodin.

"You're taking your meds, right?"

Her mom clearly didn't like the question because she didn't answer, but breathed extra hard from her tank, making it whistle like a train engine. *Phifffff-foooooo, phifffff-foooooo.* Whatever she was breathing calmed her right up.

On the coffee table in front of them was a picture of Oscar from his first and only year playing Little League football. He was wearing an oversized facemask and it hid part of his face. Crystal wished she could see his smile.

"You know, he isn't here anymore," said her mom. "I used to think he was. I know you do, too. You think he's places. Might have taken him a while to go where he goes, I know that much."

Crystal sipped her coffee and tiny bits of freeze dried grounds stuck on her tongue. She ached for a cigarette, but smoking wasn't allowed in the house, especially with Mom's oxygen tank.

"I'm just taking care of business, Mom, not letting my guard down. Trying to finish out parole so I can get out of prison for real. Have to go visit my agent today."

"After lunch, I hope?" her mom asked, and it was really a request.

"We'll see," Crystal answered back, which was really a *Sorry, I'm leaving before lunch.*

As always, lunch today would be a tomato and cheese sandwich with mayonnaise, and the morning would be spent doing small things around the house to help her mom out.

Downstairs in the laundry room, Crystal found the piles of folded laundry her mom always left there for her to carry up, two or three baskets full. She'd asked her mom more than once to let her bring the dirty clothes down, too. One fall on the stairs and Mom's hip would shatter to pieces.

Most of the morning was spent sitting in silence with her mother, looking out the picture window, listening to her mom breathe from her oxygen tank. *Phiffffff-foooooo.* Crystal waited for the right bit of awkward silence to ask for gas money. A last second request would be rude, so she had to do it soon. She couldn't find the words, so she got up to pace, thought about telling her mom how much she loved her, how much she hated everything, how scared she was and wanted everything to be okay again, but the words wouldn't come, so she went and smoked her last cigarettes on the back porch. All of them gone in quick succession.

9:30 came and both of them prepared for Crystal's uncomfortable departure.

When the doorbell rang, followed by a knock, Crystal knew it wasn't somebody selling cable. She waited for a follow-up noise to prove it was real, but nothing. Somebody was there though. She clearly saw a shadow standing at the front door.

Crystal opened the door and was looking down at Agent Hastings.

Her heart thudded in her chest. She smiled wide, trying to hide the thud, and she gave a quick glance to see if a cop car was on the street. No car in sight. If she were being arrested, Hastings would have brought two policemen, at least.

This was a surprise home visit.

"Agent Hastings," Crystal said through the screen.

"May I come in?" Hastings asked.

"I am surprised you are here. I am scheduled to see you today."

"May I?" Unlike inside the parole office, her tone was humble and professional.

"Of course. Am I still to go to the office then? This is just unusual."

"Someone's covering for me. Agent Sarkanian is taking my offenders while I make home visits instead."

Who would expect a visit on report day? Nobody, that's who. They'd have guns and drugs and mounds of coke piled high, because they'd think they were safe from a parole visit. Hastings knew the best way to catch an offender off-guard was to come on a day like this. Like all good agents, Hastings had a criminal mind.

Well, Crystal was back on her game now, and had won this round.

Hastings stepped through after permission was granted. The hobgoblin had less power here, and Crystal felt big while Hastings seemed meek.

Her mom greeted Hastings's with a smile so sweet that Crystal was sure her parole would be terminated right then. Twinkling eyes, glass of tea, a smile like a warm blanket. Hastings jumped on the chance to start the interrogation.

"Ms. Roundtree, I need to ask you a few questions about your daughter. This should only take a few minutes of your time."

"We have all morning," Mom answered. "Would you like coffee or tea, or a glass of water?"

"Nothing for me, thank you, just a few questions. You know your daughter best, you live with her, so I hope you can help me keep her out of trouble. Can you tell me if she's ever had any contact with the police, or have you ever known your daughter to associate with felons?"

"No, she just takes care of me. Works too much, I think. She likes to do hair, likes to take care of people, takes care of me. Has some new job, I think. So proud to have her paycheck, taking care of people, too. Cutting their bushes, I think, maybe even mowing lawns. She knows she needs to listen to you, I tell her but she knows. We're good here. A good life."

Mother inhaled air through her tank, *phifffff-foooooo,* taking long pauses but looking directly at Hastings without blinking. Crystal kept a straight face, didn't flinch the tiniest muscle, but was grinning on the inside. Mom knew how to lie so well, she knew how to say it, she knew what time it was, just pretended not to.

The questions kept coming,

"Have you ever known your daughter to use any illicit drugs? Has she ever left the state? Does she own any firearms? Does she caretake for any children?"

And to each one, Mom gave perfect answers with a smile, as if delighted at the interest the parole agent was showing in her. This same officer could scoop Crystal up and be sure she saw a hanging judge, but her mom was so charming that it simply wasn't going to happen.

I am free, was all Crystal could think. *I have my payroll check, surprise home visit done, might not be another for the whole parole term.* She was on her game.

They took a tour of the house, went into Crystal's room (the bed was clearly slept in. Bonus). Hastings looked in the closet, and there were enough clothes and shoes scattered there to make it look lived in. She went into the bathroom, looked in the medicine cabinet, went into the kitchen, no alcohol in the fridge. Nothing.

"Nobody else stays here but you two? No children?" Hastings asked one last, desperate time.

"Ms. Hastings," Mom said in her loudest voice. "You're the best thing could have happened to Cristi. She knows what she did was wrong, she just doesn't like telling people how she feels, but she tells me, and I know. We know our daughters."

At one point, Hastings stopped and looked at the wall of pictures. Crystal expected a frustrated Hastings to tell her "you can't have pictures of children on the wall, you've been convicted of child endangerment, and you need to take them down." But she just moved on. This was going perfect.

"Ms. Roundtree," Agent Hastings said in conclusion. "Since I had in-person contact in your home, you do not need to report. This contact will suffice. I will expect you next week."

"I have a paycheck," Crystal said, all but doing a victory dance. The tour was over. Residence confirmed. Character confirmed. Now Crystal could stick around for lunch, have a tomato and cheese sandwich with her mom, even cut the tomatoes for her, super thin, the way she liked.

The victory dance ended when a piercing shriek made Crystal's eyes wince and her spine shudder. Both Crystal and Hastings looked about the room to see where the noise was from.

It was Mom. She was gasping for oxygen, wheezing to breathe, sucking for air with all the might of her soul. Her lungs were being turned inside out.

"Mom, what is it?"

"Tank's out," Mom said. "Just stopped I think." *Pfffttt - Pffttt* – She inhaled through her nostrils, but was getting nothing out. Crystal imagined the day being destroyed by a trip to the medical supply office, but soon enough, *Phiffffff-foooooo, phifffff-foooooo,* and her mom was breathing again.

"Wait, now it's working. It's coming into me now, I think, but it smells. The air smells, like something. YUCK." She stuck out her tongue.

"It's not right. It's old, buried air. Like me. **I'M OLD, BURIED, CHOPPED APART, BURIED IN THE EARTH, SET ON FIRE.**"

A look of pain crossed her face. Her neck was shaking, and her head wouldn't stay in place. Her skin changed colors. She covered her face with her hands, all ten of her fingers trembling. Crystal moved towards her, unsure of the next step, but then her mom's eyes shot open and words of rage came firing out of her mouth:

"DO YOU KNOW WHAT SHE DOES?"

Hastings' senses came alert.

"DO YOU KNOW WHAT SHE DOES? DO YOU KNOW? SHE LIVES WITH A FELON AND SELLS HEROIN, SHE DOESN'T LIVE HERE. GO THERE AND SEE. DON'T FORGET TO CHECK FOR THE BODY IN THE BASEMENT."

Crystal could feel Hastings's brain churning, the tick of a house clock you only hear during certain kinds of silence. She needed to end this sabotage.

"Come on Mom, you've been up way too long. This is what happens. It happened yesterday, too. Mom, let's get you to bed. I'm sorry, Agent Hastings"

Crystal put an arm on her mom's shoulder. Her mom responded with a furious backhanded smack.

"SHE'S STILL LIVING ON THE SAME STREET WHERE SHE KILLED HER BOY, OSCAR. IN FACT, SHE'S GOT A BODY IN THE BASEMENT. LOCKED UP. AGAIN. THAT'S WHAT SHE DOES, SHE LOCKS KIDS UP. ALL THE WHILE SHE SELLS DOPE. LOTS AND LOTS OF DOPE."

Hastings was hypnotized at this point, nearly salivating over this disclosure with her jaw hanging to the floor. "Is what you're telling me true?"

"THE BIGGEST TRUTH YOU'LL EVER HEAR. THE BIGGEST. AND I KNOW TRUTHS. I KNOW HOW YOU GOT STABBED BACK WHEN YOU WERE A PRISON GUARD, STABBED BY A SHANK THAT DONE SLICED UP YOUR BLADDER, MAKES YOU WALK WITH A LIMP SOMETIMES, MAKES YOU WANT REVENGE ON ALL OF THEM. ALL OF THEM. WELL, ME TOO. YOU AND ME BOTH, WE NEED OUR REVENGE."

"Mom. You're delirious. Sorry, Ms. Hastings, but this is what happens. You see why I need to live here? She hasn't taken her morning medications. If she doesn't get rest, and get meds soon, we'll be back in the mental hospital. Look at all these drugs." Crystal held up the plastic bin of medications. "You see how many of these she's supposed to take? Well, she hasn't been taking them."

Hastings was puzzled. Everybody was silent, just the noises of *pfftttt---pooo, pfftttt-poooo*. Mom had stopped her madness, but with each inhale, her face turned blue. Her eyes a smoldering fire.

Crystal needed Hastings to leave.

"Ms. Roundtree," Hastings said, turning to Crystal, "we do need you to report today. We need to do a urine drop, and I do expect a discussion about this. Report today before 4:30 or you are in violation."

Discussion meant a court date, but Hastings wouldn't say that. She wouldn't want Crystal to flee.

"Of course, Agent Hastings, I can explain all of this. Maybe you can talk to my mom's doctors. Do you want my payroll check now? Or you want me to bring it to the office?"

Agent Hastings stared her down, didn't say a word, but her body pulsated with power and she was suddenly ten feet tall.

"I'm sorry about what she said," Crystal tried again. "It clearly isn't true. I hope you understand that. I know a judge wouldn't take her words as true."

"Please report today before 4:30."

Crystal watched the hobgoblin walk out the door. Her heart was shattered. She needed a joint, a cigarette, an escape plan. Everything was changed. Her mom was in her chair, and Crystal got down on her knees, face to face with her flaming eyes. "Mom, what the fuck was that? You know what you did? You just put me back in prison. Prison, Mom, and then they'll probably put you in some home. What the fuck is with you?"

"YOUR MOTHER IS GONE. SO IS LILLY. YOU'LL NEVER SEE EITHER OF THEM AGAIN."

Her mom sprung to her feet with the power of a twenty-year-old, grabbed the plastic medication bin, emptied a week's worth into her hand, and before Crystal could act, swallowed them with a dry gulp. Crystal tried to swipe the box away, but Mom smacked her hand, and emptied the whole binful of drugs down her throat. The blue of Mom's face faded to grey, her eyes rolled back into her head, and she fell lifeless on the ground.

Yes, everything was changed. Her mom had gone insane.

Crystal knelt next to her mom on the ground. She wasn't dead. Her skin was warm, her chest still rising, but Crystal needed to get her help fast. Make her throw up. Call 911. Call Poison Control. She'd seen her share of overdoses, but this was someone she loved, and maybe the only person who loved her. What the hell happened to flip her like that?

Something was wrong with the air.

Crystal took the nostril clips off her mom's nose, put them up to her own, and breathed deep.

The tank's air was putrid. Thick with death. The air burned Crystal's nostrils, coated her lungs, and then traveled to her brain. It clouded her thoughts in an instant and exploded into the words of a woman screeching:

"LILLY LIED TO YOU. SHE LIED TO YOU. OSCAR DIED A HORRIBLE DEATH. HE BURNED IN THE FLAMES. HE SCREAMED IN PAIN AND CURSED YOUR NAME. NOW HE WAITS FOR YOU IN DEATH BUT YOU'RE TOO MUCH OF A COWARD TO JOIN HIM. INSTEAD YOU TAKE A GIRL, SHOOT DRUGS IN HER VEINS, LOCK HER UP IN A BASEMENT. YOU'RE A SICK FUCK AND YOU'RE GOING BACK TO PRISON." The nostril clips clung to Crystal's nose like a parasite and she had to yank them off with both hands. She tossed the plastic tube to the ground and sucked fresh air into her lungs as fast as she could.

The tank. It was the tank that caused these massive hallucinations.

She had to act. Always act, don't get acted upon. What to do here?

First call 911, have them come and save her mother, but be gone before they get here. Rescue workers meant firemen meant policemen. Policemen would be a problem, and plus she didn't have time to wait. If she showed up at parole today, she'd be arrested, but if she didn't show up, there'd be an arrest warrant. By that time, she'd be long gone.

She had to go. She'd grab Lilly. She'd grab the money. She'd go to California. The time was now.

CHAPTER TWELVE:
JERVIS GOES TO FETCH LILLY

JERVIS MARCHED, A LONE SOLDIER, READY FOR WAR as he crossed the street. One flickering streetlight barely lit the way. The orange duffel bag was in his grasp, loaded up with Nelson's goodies. Packs of dope and the Narcan needles that Nelson was so proud of. The metal pipe, for smashing in heads, and the butcher knife, for cutting things up, clanked in the bag as well.

It was only a few weeks ago that he took this same walk across this same street and smashed in the head of the man who thought he was Lilly's father. Then he trapped Lilly in the basement, tried to burn everything down, but she stopped that somehow when she shot up the bloody mixture in her veins.

Now she was something special, and she knew she needed to live with her real father. No false dads or false lives or false hopes.

Jervis. I know where she is, Lilly's mother had said to him. **I can tell you.**

She didn't have to say much more. He knew the house with the dope. He'd been watching people walk up to the door, go inside for a moment, and then leave real fast. He waited for the right ones, nabbed them, sucked out their milk-blood, and fed it to his girl.

Now they had his girl. They had Lilly. His daughter.

I need to bring her back home. I need to fetch her, bring her home, and show her what love is. She needs to see what I did to Nelson, she'll be so happy. We'll live together like a father and daughter should.

YOU NEED TO TAKE HER APART. TAKE HER APART PIECE BY PIECE, WAKE HER UP, SKIN HER ALIVE, SHOW HER WHAT HAPPENS TO KIDS WHO DISOBEY, SHOOT HER UP INSIDE YOU. KEEP HER INSIDE YOU FOREVER.

No, Dad. No.

Jervis stared down the dope house, waiting for it to flinch. He marched up the steps of the porch, banged on the front door with his fist, and waited. Nothing. He pounded again, the noise echoing inside his skull. The itch on his neck started to burn and he longed for the knife in his bag.

THE ITCH WON'T STOP UNTIL YOU GET HER

He sensed movements on the other side of the door. An eyeball in the peephole. Multiple clicks of bolts being undone, and then the door swung open.

A gun was pointed straight at his eyes. He couldn't help but blink.

"What the fuck are you?" the man asked. "What the hell do you want? Tell me before I blow your fucking head off."

"My girl. I know she's here."

"Your girl? Your girl? You mean Zach's kid, huh? You know about her. Yeah, maybe I got her, so what?"

"I need her back."

The gun dropped a bit, aimed at his chest, not his head. The man shifted his weight back and forth and looked both ways down the street.

"You don't get her for free. Five hundred. You got that much, and she's yours."

"Yeah, I got that."

The man smiled, dropped the gun another inch, and widened his feet as if guarding the entrance.

"What the fuck is wrong with your head?"

The man squinted his eyes and crunched up his nose. Confusion came out of his skin and mixed with the traces of so many dope fiends who'd been there before.

And his daughter, his girl, was trapped inside. Nobody could just come and take what's his.

"Got what you want, I do."

Jervis reached into his bag and dug around, the gun ready to fire at his head if he did the wrong thing. *That don't matter, this man has no idea who I am.* Once his hands felt the cold steel of the metal pipe, he swung it out of the bag and it smacked into both gun and hand.

A shot fired. Jervis felt the burning stab of a bullet glance off his shoulder, but the gun had been knocked to the floor. Surprise filled the dope man's face. Jervis started smashing it with the pipe. The metal crushed his nose first, then the flat bone of his temple, then the fragile side of jaw, then his eye socket which caved in quickly. His body dropped.

"You think you can take her?" Jervis yelled. "You think you can sell her? You don't know what kind of Poppa the girl has. Where is she?"

Silence. Nothing.

Damnit. He took too many swings. The man couldn't talk back. Only thing coming out of his swollen, purple lips was blood and teeth.

Jervis stepped inside, waiting to see what else was alive in this house and who he had to battle to win his daughter back. Nobody was in sight, but he knew that a woman lived there, too. She must be around, but there was no woman. Just an old couch, an older coffee table, shoes on the floor, and a ratty blue blanket hanging on the front window. He paced back and forth into each and every room, waiting to see Lilly with each step.

No Lilly, just rats dashing back and forth, too fast to track. A picture of a young boy hung on the wall and watched him. The big TV in one bedroom was laughing at him.

Where is she?

The house had been searched, his insides were empty, his itch burned, and then the customers came in swarms. So many of them came through the front door, all of them looking for dope. Greasy, soiled beings with saliva dripping from their mouths, sweat beads on their foreheads, snot on their nose, wet shit from their ass, their bodies dripping and leaving trails of themselves. All of them looking to end their illness and get a fix. Each of them looking to take a tiny chunk of his daughter.

YOU NEED A TINY CHUNK, TOO. OH GOD, WILL IT GIVE YOU THE HIGHS OF ALL THE HEAVENS.

Jervis paced back and forth so fast his brain swirled around in his skull. He dug his knife into his itch and felt his brain stem ready to sever. He needed a fix, his own fix, or his daughter.

Where is she?

She's under me, of course. That's where she goes. Basements.

The night of the fire, it was a basement he'd locked her inside of, and that's where she must be now.

He found the basement door, twisted the handle and pulled, but it was stuck. There was a padlock on the door jamb. He yanked so hard on the doorknob that the house shook and dust fell from above, but he could not get in. The lock was solid. He swung with the pipe and the crashing noise cut into his ears, but the lock would not give.

"Lilly! Lilly!" he yelled over and over while banging on the door.

She'd be in her sleep, hurting. He knew what it was like to be trapped in a basement and hurting. His mom had locked him in for days, and the pain of having no dope ate him alive. That wouldn't happen to his own daughter.

The gun. He retrieved it from the front room carpet, and one quick aim and pull of the trigger and the metal padlock broke free from the splintered door jamb. One more shot and it fell to the ground.

"Lilly."

He walked down the stairs. The air was damp, everything burned, but he could feel her spirit in the depths.

There she was, flat on her back next to the yellow glow of a nightlight. Her eyes were closed and her face was twisted up and stuck that way. She'd been bathed—her hair was still wet and her charcoal flesh glistened like diamonds in the nightlight.

AND YOU CAN PEEL IT BACK PIECE BY PIECE. YOU THINK MY ASHES GOT YOU HIGH? IMAGINE THIS PIECE OF BEAUTY JAMMED UP INTO YOUR VEINS.

She needed to wake up and open her eyes. Those white ovals, each one of them a God to him. He carried her up the basement stairs. She was weightless, as if empty.

He laid her on the ground and shuffled through the orange duffel bag. What to do next?

Fix up some of Nelson's good dope. Save her. Stop her suffering. Bring her back home, make her feel safe.

NO. CUT HER UP. BOIL THE PIECES, THEN SHOOT THEM UP. RIGHT INTO YOUR VENTRICLE.

She was so tiny in front of him, just a small piece of his own flesh. The only part of him that would ever matter. Her skin was like none other. Her body had the milk-blood of some of the harshest addicts the city had known.

What to do next?

The house and all the ghosts of addicts who'd been inside waited on his decision.

Maybe Dad was right. She would want to be inside of me. She would understand why. There must be so much dope in her body.

THERE IS. THERE IS.

Maybe I can start taking pieces, soak them, boil them, shoot them.

YOU CAN. YOU CAN.

Footsteps on the front porch stopped his thoughts. He turned to the doorway, and saw a figure standing there. Looking at him.

"I know you. I've seen you here before," Jervis said. "You're coming back here when you shouldn't. You should go. You don't want to see this. Go before I kill you, too."

But the person didn't leave, and Jervis would have to do battle again.

CHAPTER THIRTEEN:
CRYSTAL'S ESCAPE TO CALIFORNIA

HER MOM WAS BREATHING WHEN SHE LEFT. Crystal made sure of that. And she was resting comfortably. Her face was clammy, pale, and she didn't respond to soft slaps on the cheek, but, *she was breathing when I left.* These were the words she'd have to tell a detective if she were ever interviewed for "elderly endangerment charges," if there was such a thing.

She will not die. She's breathing. Shallow, yes, but breathing. Pill bottles were on the table for 911 rescue workers to know exactly what she'd overdosed on. Crystal would call the hospital anonymously later to see how her mother was doing.

You are the same kind of bad that Hastings thinks you are. Leaving her alone.

No, it would be fine, and she was doing the right thing. She had to do this, and she would do it right, make the right moves. Hastings had the ball rolling to put her back in prison. She'd have a policeman waiting to arrest her at the parole office. Best case scenario would be staying out of jail until a court date with Judge Donaldson, but Donaldson and Hastings spoke as one.

Her fingers fumbled through the ashtray, looking for a cigarette butt to smoke, but they'd all been smoked down to the filter. Goddamn did she need a cigarette, or a joint. Something to strike some lightning in her cloudy head.

No smokes and no gas in her car. The gauge wasn't even pointing at E anymore, but jiggling to the left of the E. And she had no license plate, but she'd fix both of those things. She'd get money to gas up when she got home. Dials on these cars never work, there's always way more gas than it shows. The escape plan needed her focus.

And you're leaving Oscar behind?

No, I'm taking Oscar with me. Lilly is Oscar.

If Avanti wasn't home, it would be easy. She'd grab all of her cash, and take whatever cash Vanti didn't have locked up. Where he hid most of it, she wasn't sure, but she knew where the dope was. She'd take a big chip. Enough to get her through until she got settled. Whatever city they ended up in, she'd find more dope—every city has a Brentwood Street. She'd see to it to take care of her new child.

Next she'd screw her license plate back on, grab some food, then grab Lilly. The body from the basement would be last, wrapped in a blanket. She'd look like the fireman who had carried her dead child, Oscar, out of a house years ago. She'd gas up and leave this city, take I-94 past Chicago, she already knew the way, then I-80 through states like Iowa and Nebraska, driving the speed limit, doing everything she could to avoid a DWB until she got to the western shores. The edge of the world.

But if Avanti was home, and he probably would be, she'd need an excuse to gather her things.

"I saw Hastings, it went okay," she would tell him, *"but you're right, we don't need that skinny skeleton in our basement. I'm going to dump it in the field right now."*

She'd have to be convincing, and then make sure he didn't follow her into the bedroom so she could grab the baggies of dope and stacks of cash. As for Lilly, he'd be happy to know that Zach's kid was being dumped in a field. He wouldn't wonder what happened until she'd been gone for hours.

How long until he'd care that she'd left him? And how long until Oscar would care? Could she really just leave Oscar behind?

She drove slow, deliberately. Brake lights in front of her pulsated with their own heartbeat. Everything was alive, watching her. Her insides were churning. Her eyes were radar, looking for danger, the feeling of the steering wheel acute on her fingers. She hadn't eaten, and her body was grasping for energy, trying to move on, and the car itself followed suit. It sputtered, gave a jerky response.

Pfftt-pooo. She pushed the pedal furiously, all the way to the floor, but no response. The car was refusing her.

Gas was gone. She pounded the steering wheel with her fists and guided the car to the side of the road, as close to the curb as she could put it.

Emergency blinkers? No, she didn't want anybody to stop. What to do next?

There was an intersection within sight and she could see a Shell gas station with the yellow clam on the sign. She just needed one dollar of gas to get her home. Somebody would help.

She was still on her game, she had this. There was a gas can in the trunk, all was not lost. She'd fix this fast. When she opened the trunk, leftover gas fumes greeted her.

She walked briskly down the street, holding the gas can high in one hand, signaling it was weightless and empty, hoping somebody might offer to help. Cars drove by, many of them beeping at her, one giving her the middle finger.

She made it to the Shell station. A sign read FREE COFFEE WITH AN 8 GALLON FILLUP. Trash cans were overfull and the parking lot was crowded. This would be easy.

She scanned faces, read body language, looking for the right person. At any minute a cop car could pull behind hers, notice no plates, and have more questions than Crystal could ever answer. And as soon as she didn't show up at probation, an arrest warrant would be issued.

Hastings had no idea what type of action people like her would take. She had never known how much love she had for Oscar. Crystal would be in Kalamazoo by the time Hastings was expecting her, and would never be back.

And Oscar will be forgotten. His tombstone of a house will be desecrated and sink further and further into Hell. Can Lilly even talk to Oscar if you take her so far away?

Drivers pulled into the gas station, self-absorbed, avoiding her eyes. They parked by the pumps, refueled, and went back to their lives. She kept the gas can visible to make her plight obvious. Those with the best cars might be first to help.

A Ford Expedition rode up and a woman stepped out in a hurry. Crystal got ready to ask for help but stopped when she saw a cell phone at her ear. The woman was smoking a cigarette, inhaled deep, and then blew the smoke back into the heavens. She let the cigarette drop to the ground, gave it a pat with her shoe and walked inside the station.

Crystal felt her mouth water, her lungs ached, and after the woman was gone, she picked the cigarette butt up off the ground. The paper wasn't broken and the filter was intact. She stuck it in her mouth, tasted the woman's lips, relit the tip with her green Bic lighter, and filled her lungs.

Ahhhh.

"You're one gross muthafucker."

The man's voice came from behind her. She turned, half expecting a cop, but it was no cop. A yellow shirt clung tight to his large, basketball belly. His face was camouflaged by a thick beard. He held the gas nozzle at his truck and looked her body up and down. She'd let it go for a dollar's worth of gas.

"Have you got just a touch to spare? Please sir, I really need it?" she held the gas can forward.

"Whatchu need it for?" He squinted suspiciously.

"My son. He's waiting for me at home. All alone. I got to get to him. My car isn't far."

It wasn't far, she could see it on the side of the road, and tried pointing it out, but he wasn't looking.

"Son my ass," he answered. A devil grin spread between his fat cheeks. "Let me guess. You ran out of gas and need money. Your son is stranded and waiting for you somewhere else."

"Yes. He's stranded, and I need to get back to him. It's been a long time."

"What's his name? Say it fast without thinking."

"Oscar."

"Humph," the man grunted, rolled his eyes, turned to walk away, and then changed his mind.

"Bullshit. You don't even have a kid named Oscar. And if you do, he doesn't care one shit about you. You're a junky alcoholic lying motherfucker, aren't you? Did you work today? Do you work at all? You sit here and lie to people. I work hard for my money while you lie about some son of yours to cheat me out of it."

"I am not lying."

"Okay. I'll give you some gas and you show me. You take me to him."

An offer for gas, how could she say no?

"You sure about that?"

"Hell yeah. I'll give you some gas, and you let me see him. But when he's not there, I stomp my boots across your grill. Here, take it."

He presented the nozzle for Crystal to take, and she grabbed it firmly. The gas pump showed fifty-three dollars had already gone in his tank. Fifty-three damn dollars for his car. That didn't happen where she came from. You fill up five bucks at a time when you grew up on Brentwood. You live near vacant houses, abandoned by all except crackheads and ghosts, bars on the window for the living, where Molotov cocktails show up on your doorstep as much as any piece of mail.

She peered at her car, a quarter mile down the road. It sat there, sad, stranded, dead, but ready to be brought back to life. Her car, Lilly, both of them were comatose and relying on her for fuel. Time to go. To act. To be on top of her game and escape to California.

She unscrewed the top of the gas can, staring at her car in the distance, and started to fill.

As if in response, a black and white cop car, lights on top, cop inside, pulled up to her bumper. The front door opened, and the uniformed cop got out.

The heavens crashed down from the sky. Hell erupted from the earth. Her plan was shot

No. You can explain to the policeman why you have no plate, you can show him your ID, there's no arrest warrant yet, you're still golden. Get out of here. Gas up the car, dope up the child, flee.

But who would bring her to life? What would take care of her? Nothing. Nobody. Everything she wanted was dead or out of reach, and once she made the run to California, even farther away.

The nozzle grew heavy and she stopped pumping. Her vision tinted red, jaw dropped, tongue dried, and insides imploded. Voices of her past whispered about prison, about leaving Oscar. The whispers became screams; Oscar yelling for help inside his locked room, burning in the flames and cursing her name, nobody to hear him ever again. The sickly girl with the dope habit locked in the basement cried in the background.

Loudest of all was the voice she had heard just hours earlier.

HE'S WAITING FOR YOU BUT YOU'RE TOO MUCH OF A COWARD TO JOIN HIM.

"I knew it," the fat man grunted. "You don't have a real son, do you? You're no mother."

Crystal looked into the eyes of the fat man while she turned the nozzle straight to herself and sprayed her body with gas. It dripped down her chest and was colder than she thought it would be. Thick fumes traveled into her eyes, up her nose, and down her throat.

Whites of the fat man's eyes grew wide. His face dripped from suspicion to fear. She turned the nozzle and sprayed his yellow shirt. It was soaked instantly and clung tight to his round belly. She flicked her green Bic lighter before he could escape.

Both of them burst like logs on a bonfire. The flame sizzled her skin and followed the fumes up her nostrils and down her throat. The burning fat man dashed about the parking lot, but not Crystal. She bathed in the flames, scorching her body inside and out. Her flesh melted and her organs bubbled into liquid. Her bones could hold up no longer and she fell to the ground. The flames melted her flesh off her body and kept harrowing deeper until they burst her soul into full orgasm.

This was what Oscar really felt. Oscar did burn—maybe not by flames, but by the smoke that was thick and hot and had boiled him alive. Lilly had indeed lied to her, but it was okay. She lied because she cared.

Crystal was finally okay. The locks were broken and her soul was released. She was going back to her son, dying and burning like he did—same kind of ashes, same kind of death.

Both of them going to where all smoke rises.

CHAPTER FOURTEEN:
LILLY HEARING VOICES OF THE DEAD IN THE DARKNESS OF HER SLEEP

YOU DON'T EVEN KNOW WHAT'S HAPPENING, DO YOU? THAT WOMAN WHO PUT YOU DOWN HERE IS DEAD AND NEVER COMING BACK. YOUR POPPA JERVIS IS TRYING TO LOVE YOU, BUT HE CAN'T BECAUSE YOU AREN'T LOVABLE. YOU HAVEN'T BEEN LOVABLE SINCE THE DAY YOU WERE IN ME. YOU WERE JUST A ROTTING PEACH PIT POPPA INJECTED INTO MY GUT, AND NOTHING'S CHANGED. NOW HE'S GOING TO CARVE YOU INTO TINY PIECES. YOU THINK THE FLAMES YOU FEEL IN YOUR INSIDES HURT NOW? THAT'S NOTHING. THIS WILL HURT, AND IT WILL LAST, AND WHEN IT IS FINALLY OVER, YOU'LL BE PART OF HIS INSIDES FOREVER.

Lilly. It's me. I did it. I found Oscar. Thank you. Thank you.

CHAPTER FIFTEEN:
DWIGHT COMES BACK

FITTING INSIDE THE CAR WAS NOT EASY. He was walking with a crutch under one armpit, and his left leg in a long cast. The driver's seat was pulled back, and his right leg had to push forward to reach the gas. Each bump rattled his bones, threatening to shake them loose. He'd been bandaged up so much, he looked like a Halloween mummy on the way to a party.

Dwight wasn't supposed to be leaving the house right now. He'd promised he would just stay on the couch when his parents finally left him alone. As soon as they left, he started his plan. Things had to be done. Things he'd been promising himself over the last six days in the hospital bed.

If he'd told the full truth to the detectives maybe they'd have found the killer, but Dwight didn't want himself incriminated. Didn't want his drug habit to be discovered. Ever since it happened, his entire world had been split apart, and the metal rod put into his leg was holding it together. Another surgery was coming. The tiny dosage of pain killers they gave him weren't taking away memories of what happened to him on Brentwood.

Next to the crutch on the passenger seat, was his dad's pistol. He had mimicked shooting in his hand so many times that he felt he'd done it already. It would be as natural as pointing a finger. He was going to shoot things. Kill things on the street. He wasn't even sure who. The beast of a man who killed Brian and then cut Dwight up and shattered his tibia would be the first. Next person would be the drug dealer who tricked him into injecting heroin. He pictured both of them with a bullet wound on their forehead.

Not sure who else he was going to kill, but it didn't matter. The street is a place you're allowed to kill. Nobody cares around there, and the place needed some cleansing. It was full of death, bodies, and demon-looking dolls that talk to you. Nobody knew this if they didn't go there, but he did, and he also knew about the treasures. How much heroin must be inside that house.

But he wasn't going for the heroin, never again. He had prayed for God to "just get me out of here safely and I'll never get high again," and God answered his prayers.

Then again, someone who hurt as much as he did would be forgiven for using just a little heroin to get him by. The pain in his leg was searing, the metal rod inside continually stabbing him.

Vengeance was his new high. That's why he was going back to Brentwood. To do what was right. If he got high, to kill some pain, that was just collateral. He was not going to be an addict anymore. He wasn't an addict, in fact, and he would keep his promise to God for keeping him alive.

When he saw the street sign, Brentwood, it made every bone, broken or not, tingle inside him.

He parked curbside, groaned at the pain getting out of the car and prepared to be attacked as soon as he opened the door. Instead, the street was quiet, dark, all of it asleep, a place birds don't even chirp at the morning light, where crickets don't sing. Soon as he saw the dope house, he remembered that golden high from the shot of heroin.

But that's not why I am here. I am here for justice, not the heroin.

Where to go first? The house where the monster had attacked him was full dark. The front door was a menacing grin, the second floor window a hypnotizing eye.

But the drug dealer's house had lights on, and the front door was wide open.

Open in the middle of the night. Who knows why? Maybe he should just scout it out and not attack tonight, but the longer he stood and watched and breathed the air from this street, the more he became part of it. The small voice in his head telling him to stop completely vanished.

He walked up the sidewalk, crutch under one armpit, gun in the other hand, trigger finger itchy. Getting up the porch steps wasn't easy, but with an open door, he felt invited.

Standing in the doorway, the guts of the house came into focus. It was clear something unusual had happened here this night. He could feel it first—then he could see it.

On the ground, not far inside the doorway, the body of the drug dealer lie as if waiting for a chalk outline. His face was a familiar mess of swollen purple, same as Brian's had been. Blood freshly streamed from his eyes and nose, but his life was over. That was evident.

And the cause of it was clear, too, for standing deeper in the house was the monster, working over the demon doll he had brought to life.

This was perfect. Dwight felt a glow of pride and stood there unnoticed at first, while the beast rustled through a bag of goodies next to him. The man's lips were mumbling words, speaking in tongues and talking as if in conversation with voices unheard. He was debating with himself, no idea he was being observed. The gash in his neck was even bigger; tendons dangled like wires, and his head seemed ready to fall to the ground, but apparently he could still speak.

"I know you. I've seen you here before," the beast said when he finally noticed Dwight. "You're coming back here when you shouldn't. You should go. You don't want to see this. Go before I kill you, too."

Dwight felt little fear, and would not be ordered this time. He had a gun, he was in charge.

He raised the pistol and fired one shot. The monster jerked back, paused, but two more shots and the monster was grounded.

Dwight stepped inside. All was silent now, and he looked down at the girl. Dead on the ground, it seemed, but he'd seen her like this before. Then she came back to life. He aimed the gun at her body and wanted to shoot her in the head until her skull chipped right off, but stopped. She was the one who let him go, she was not the enemy here, but a victim.

What to do next?

He wondered if policemen and ambulances would be coming after the gunfire, but there was nothing. No noises, no sirens. Finally he heard footsteps behind him and swiveled on his feet.

"Don't shoot. Don't shoot," said the man behind him with arms outstretched. "No need to shoot, okay? I'm not here for anything you want. Not here for you."

A skinny white man. A dope customer. Unbathed, pale skin, clammy, and certainly not a threat. Dwight did lower the gun.

The man walked straight past him inside the house, looked about for a moment, and then knelt down next to the charbroiled girl. He mumbled under his breath, nervous ticks spasmed in his face, not much different than the beast he'd just put down.

"I'm going to take her. I've been following her for a long time. I know what happened to you. I'm sorry I didn't do something. You weren't the only one, but maybe the only one to survive it all."

"I'm taking her," he said again as he picked the demon-doll up and cradled her across his arms. The man walked by, and when Dwight smelled the stench of her body, it brought back his whole sad, tragic week. Dope and needles, his body being destroyed, his leg ripped apart, the monster who killed Brian. It made him sick. Turmoil in his gut pulled at his throat. He got ready to vomit but nothing came forth, it only settled back down into his gut, its new home. His whole self was becoming wretched, and he was sure his insides looked like this girl's outsides. Where he was taking this girl, Dwight didn't want to know.

"You better get out of here," the man said before he walked off. "Things here will get you. Stick around here one minute longer and you may never leave."

The man was gone, Dwight was left, the sole survivor. The winner.

He didn't have to look long before finding some heroin in the house. Right on the ground was an orange duffel bag with fresh syringes, packs of dope, and needles labeled Narcan inside. He wasn't sure how to fix up, but he'd seen it done plenty of times, and went to the kitchen to do his best. Water and heroin mixed on a spoon, heating the metal until the mixture boiled, sucked it up into the syringe, drawing some blood from his veins, pushing in, and then *ahhhhhhh,* all that time was worth it. His leg didn't ache, life was grand, and he could go home a better man.

He took two steps to the front door when he heard someone speak.

"You should have listened. You should have got out of here."

The monster had risen. Gunshot wounds on his chest were fresh and bloody. Shards of vertebrae stuck out of his neck.

There was no going home for Dwight that night.

The shrieks of pain spilling out of the house lasted for hours but went unheeded. It didn't matter how much Dwight screamed for help. And it didn't matter what kind of pain the monster inflicted, Dwight could not answer the question he was asked again and again, a question that, if he could have answered, might have ended the torture:

"Where is my daughter, where did she go?"

He had no idea, so the pain was inflicted for as long as Dwight's heart continued to beat.

His last thoughts were promises to God to never come back to Brentwood if he could just make it home alive.

God couldn't help him anymore.

The End.
* * * * * *

YOU PUT THE PAGES DOWN. You've read them straight through without a break, and wonder if you've read them all. You search the bag that the body was brought in, but there are no more words for you to read. All that's left are the two bodies.

The patient from the hospital, the one who brought Lilly here, the one who wrote this story, has killed himself in your house. His blood coats your floor like spilled mop water.

You breathe. You think about cleaning the blood, you think about covering the body with a blanket, but you can't move. A shower is what you want. Maybe if you let the warm water scald your body long enough and stand in the steam with eyes closed, when you emerge, all of this will be gone.

You still need to call 911. EMTs, firemen, police, all of them will arrive to witness what you are seeing is real. They've seen things like this before, but this one will burn in their memories a bit longer than most.

Call 911.

But not just yet. You are meant to do something here, but what is it? This man brought her here for a reason. Did he expect you to start feeding this girl heroin? That was not going to happen. Even if you could believe what you read as truth, you would not inject heroin into her body.

You put a finger against Lilly's neck. Nothing. Dead is dead, but her flesh isn't as frigid as a cadavers should be. The skin is a rugged hide, and if a heart is beating softly underneath, you can't feel it through the thick shell the girl was trapped inside.

You do call 911 and ask for help. Then you sit in the somber stillness, and wait.

Soon enough, police and ambulance lights are twirling outside. Men in uniform come through the door and ask you questions. They offer you help. They suggest you go to the hospital, but you decline. They take pictures, more people come, they ask you the same questions, you give the same answers.

You walk the first responders out the door. They recommend a hotel, you politely thank them. The birds are chirping before the ambulance has gone, with the body inside.

But they have not taken away Lilly's body.

You hid her well before calling 911. She's deep in your basement, inside a closet and covered by blankets, like secrets you've compartmentalized so deep in your brain. Had they discovered that you hid her, you would have been brought in for questioning, and your answers would not have been sufficient. You'd be in jail. But they know nothing of Lilly, nor did you show them the manuscript. You've kept that safe. All they know is one of your patients came to your house, broke in, and committed suicide.

Within twenty-four hours, SharePoint offers you a paid leave of absence, and promises to do a full investigation into why an actively suicidal patient was discharged, and how that patient found your home. You're not sure you will ever return to work. The blood will never be clean. A new floor is needed.

You're not sleeping at night. The moment you slip into a dream there's a clamoring of screeches from behind the blackness, nothing you can make out, and nothing that lasts, since the sound wakes you quickly. You're waiting for another insane man to crash through the front window in the middle of the night. Each night that he doesn't come is followed by a morning where you go downstairs and check to be sure Lilly's body is there. You can see her body clearly, right where you left it, but you wish you could find a witness to confirm its truth.

You do know there is a Brentwood. You've mapped it, and if the man named Jervis won't come to you, then someday you may go to him.

Each morning over coffee you wonder what you will do with the body in your basement. You decide not to return to work and put in your resignation. When you go to gather your things, you spend some time in Medical Records looking up charts from the last decade.

As expected, you find the name you were looking for: Jervis Samsa.

He was admitted on September 22nd, eight years ago. The Detroit Capuchin soup kitchen brought him in; disheveled, psychotic, responding to voices, paranoid delusions. You kept him for a seventy-two hour hold, then another seventy-two hours, but once he was fully detoxed, once he showed no signs of responding to internal stimuli, denied self-harm, denied harm to others, was medication compliant, he was discharged and referred to a community mental health facility. Very standard, low maintenance case. Same as a dozen others that month.

There are hundreds of Jervis Samsas out there, but this one did more damage than most.

You did it. You let him live.

The impact of your decision remains as a body in your basement. At times you go down there, ready to find a way to discard it properly, but often you notice it has moved slightly, the left leg with its knee bent rather than straight. The head tilted to the side rather than looking at the ceiling. A hand over her heart when you had left it at her side.

But staring at the body for six hours straight, you never see it move. You have tried. And with all that staring, you have come to know it well. You could draw it from memory: the small pug nose, the mouth stuck in a Mona Lisa grimace. Arms and legs with charcoal skin sewed on over bone, a blackened rawhide set of armor, the slight stench of singed hair, but the trace of lavender shampoo when you pinch a strand and sniff.

And the track marks of heroin injections, too many to count, pecked all over her like a million dot to dots.

"What do you want, Lilly?" you ask under your breath. "What do you need me to do? Tell me, give me a sign, and I'll do it."

Nothing. If you believe what you read, she is being burnt alive inside her black cocoon and mocked by voices of the dead. Whatever is inside this shell needs to be set free. But how?

There it was, in the title of the story. What the man wanted when he brought her body here.

Where All Smoke Rises

Your decision is made. You wait three days, none of them eventful, to see if your mind changes. It does not. You take the body out of your basement in the darkness of 4 a.m., carry it back beyond where your lawn is mowed, and you gather brush to form a pyre.

You pour the gas around her—not on the body, that seems too much—but on the sticks of trees and foliage. The moon is a giant glowing eye and the only witness to your backyard cremation. If neighbors weren't so far off, they would see this clear as day under the moonlight glow, but you bought this house for its seclusion, and there isn't a human in sight.

You wish ten-year-old Lilly could have family here to see this. Someone who loved her from birth. But perhaps nobody did. She was always alone. Strangers like you were the ones meant to care for her, but did not. You feel strangely responsible. Best you can do now is destroy the body that has kept her soul captive and suffering.

You wonder if she knows what's about to happen.

You have a box of matches, but wait to strike, letting the moment alone. The world is completely still. The universe is holding its breath as you watch over Lilly's body. The celestial silver shines off her charcoal skin, making it glisten like tiny diamond crystals. You see how beautiful her black cocoon is through this silver moonlight.

And that's when a metal pipe from a two-handed swing strikes you on the bottom of your rib cage, sending you sprawling on the ground. All the breath is knocked from your lungs. Your rib is cracked, seems to be sticking into your lung. You gasp for air but nothing comes. Your wind has been smashed out of you.

"Burn her? That's what you think? That's what you do to show her some love? You're the same kind of bad as me."

Jervis Samsa is standing before you, with a voice belting louder than you'd imagined when reading his dialogue. His body radiates heat, his head leans to one side, just as you read, only now it's absurdly so. Just tiny threads are keeping it attached.

"I know why he brought her to you. I know why. You were one of them doctors. One of them who kept me in the hospital, said I was crazy, but I told you different. I told you I wasn't hearing them voices. I took the pills you gave me, and you let me go."

Jervis paces with frantic steps. The orange duffel bag hangs over his arms. His lips move as fast as his legs, murmuring words, talking, then pausing, having a conversation with someone in his head, but not with you. It finally ends and he screams at your face.

"But now, DOCTOR. Now YOU regret it. Now YOU see what I'm about to do. Fathers LOVE their daughters, that's what they DO. But YOU wouldn't know about all that, about how WE do these things..."

Jervis reaches into his bag and you move to stop him, but before you can, he's acted. His hand raises an object in the air and then slams it down, stabbing it into Lilly's body. He grunts in satisfaction, waits, then pulls out.

"But that ain't all. It's just the beginning. There's more."

Another object from the bag, raised again in the air, and he stabs Lilly again, hard enough you can hear her flesh being punctured. His hand moves fast. She's being butchered, her body being punctured again and again. He jabs in, pulls out and you scream but words won't come, only noises. The rib stuck in your lung stops your voice.

Jervis finally stops on his own and stands over her.

"This. This is it," he says, holding up what you realize is a needle.

"Narcan. I didn't know nothing about Narcan, but Nelson sure did. Just one brought him back from the dead—a dozen or so might just do the trick for Lilly. We'll see."

Jervis steps back, paces, mumbles some more, then finally says something you can understand.

"I ain't ready to shave her down, to cut her up, to inject her into my veins. That ain't love. But my daddy keeps asking. Keeps asking me to and he won't stop. I've had enough. I'm done here."

He pulls out a huge knife from his bag and begins sawing at the base of his own head. His jaw hangs slack and his efforts are futile, for you know his neck vertebra is too much to be cut through, but you're wrong. The stem's been weakened and it breaks off easily. His head hits the ground like a giant acorn going *thump*. His body tumbles beside it.

You feel his hate lift, a nighttime fog dissipating in the dark, the moonlight free to glisten with glory. But Lilly remains in the pyre.

You crawl to her side, stand over her, just a helpless doctor. She's been ripped open by a dozen punctures in her body left by Jervis. The stench of gas hits your nose, waiting to be lit, but the fire inside your brain is already burning.

Something on her body moves. Her limbs are in motion but the shell she's trapped in is cracking. The tiny charred pieces begin breaking off, just little bits, and they rise from her body like the fruit flies from your kitchen. Bigger pieces, more of them, buzzing in circles and lifting in the air.

Underneath it is flesh. Nearly human. A young black female, gaunt, bluish tint to her fingertips and lips. So skinny you could see her ribs, so frail she needs an intensive care unit, but it has worked. She's alive.

Lilly has emerged.

She leans forward and a shrieking cry comes from deep in her chest, the pain of a thousand children's deaths, screeching so long that you can't believe the sky doesn't shatter and the moon doesn't come crashing down. Each time the screech seems over, it starts back up, louder and at a higher pitch, until finally her thundering cry fades to fragile sobs, and wet tears stream down her face.

You embrace her, pulling her slight body into your chest, her whole body heaving, gasping for breath, crying the pain of her soul from her eyes. Her tears don't stop, and she is your only patient, your only concern, and you try to transfer the comfort of your soul onto hers. You want to say you're sorry, you want to tell her it will get better, but all you can do is show her. And make it happen.

Hours pass. The moonlight vanishes on the horizon and the sun gets ready to peek from the East. But before it does, and before you take her inside, you have a fire to light.

Lilly watches as if she knows what needs to be done as you pull the headless carcass of Jervis back over the funeral pyre. You kick along his severed heard with your foot, add more gas, and both of you watch him burn while the sun rises.

You return home, holding her hand as she walks with steps unsteady. You give her juice. Each drink she swallows makes her cough, but soon as the cough ends, she drinks more. You wrap up her shaking body with an afghan blanket and sit with her until she falls asleep on the couch.

This time, you feel a heartbeat when you place a finger at her neck, and warm breaths from her nostrils.

Days go on. At night you go out back to where Jervis's charred body lies. Each time you add a bit more gas, do a bit more burning, enough so that you can garden-hoe his body into ashes and then bury them. It would take a DNA test to prove a body was ever there.

Lilly is still in your basement at night. She has tried to sleep elsewhere, but likes it down there best. There's a TV beside the futon you set up, but it's never used. She's homeschooled a bit, is overly obedient, and says little. Once in a while tiny bits of emotions slip out, bits of gratitude even, that might go unnoticed if you weren't looking. You want to find the spark to make her glow again.

That is your job now, to make her glow again. You'll cash in your 401k, downsize your house, and move to where nobody knows a thing of either of you.

And you do need to move. Maybe as far as the edges of California, for more than once, she has come up from her spot in the basement in the dark of night, when neither of you can see each other's faces, and speaks with fear.

"The ashes. Poppa Jervis's ashes. They're speaking to me, asking me to inject them, and I can't stop thinking about it, what it would feel like. It keeps me awake at night."

Acknowledgements

First a few words about the city of Detroit. While some of the urban decay and poverty is actually understated in the MILK-BLOOD books, much of Detroit is growing and becoming a wonderful place. Best theater district outside of Broadway, a downtown where occupancy is so high, young hipsters wait in line for new lofts, and new businesses are flooding downtown all the time. On summer nights, when a baseball game or concert lets out and people fill the streets and music fills the air, it's a wonderful place. Abandoned houses are being bulldozed by the hundreds, neighborhoods are starting to grow again, urban farming is taking root, and the perseverance of Detroit is thriving. These novels could have taken place in any city occupied by humans.

The addiction as described in these books is all too real. Heroin and opiate addiction is an epidemic. One hundred people per day from combined heroin and opiate overdoses. That's four every hour. If it took you three hours to read this, then twelve people died while you read (more than died in the book). Substance abuse treatment does work. I've seen it and lived it, and Narcan is a very real life-saving substance that reverses opioid overdoses and is now being carried by many police officers in major cities.

I saved Lilly at the end of this book, partly in response to both public and private comments about the fatalistic nature of things I have written. I do believe in the glory and grace of the human spirit, but the dark corners of this world are too often ignored. Our lights shine brightest in this darkness. The light will never win this endless war, but always wins the battles.

I want to thank so many who have helped me with this book, including Julie Hutchings, for her stellar job at editing. Kealan Patrick Burke, for writing an introduction that gave me goosebumps. John F.D. Taff, for his digital mentorship. Richard Thomas, who edited Milk-Blood and has been a tremendous help over the years. Jason Parent, for bouncing around ideas for All Smoke Rises. Charlene from Goodreads, for moderating Horror Aficionados, (the best Goodreads reading group there is.) Also a huge thanks to the wonderful beta readers, including Andi Rawson, Janie C., Michael Fowler, David Spell, and Barbara Tsipouras, who have really helped shape this book.

Finally, thanks to my wife and children for putting up with me in my obsessed state. Nothing I have ever written hasn't been driven by an obsessiveness that keeps me preoccupied and maniacally driven until it is finished. I too often check out when trapped in the world of my fiction.

Part of the reason for this obsession is that these stories become true as I write them. In fact, I invite you to come by and I shall show you where Jervis is buried. His ashes are free for you to inject. Lilly's California address remains a secret, but I am happy to report she sees a doctor regularly, is receiving treatment for cyanosis, and is currently learning to cope with heroin cravings. One day at a time.

About the Author.

Mark Matthews is the author of five novels, including *On The Lips of Children*, which was a number one selling horror novel on Amazon and published by Books of the Dead Press. MILK-BLOOD: Part one, was optioned for a full length feature film and was a 2015 Best Kindle Book Awards Semi-Finalist. All of his novels are based on true settings, many of them inspired by his work as a counselor in the field of mental health and treatment of addiction. He is the editor of, and contributing author to, Garden of Fiends and Lullabies for Suffering. He's a member of the Horror Writers Association, has run over a dozen marathons, and has a Bachelor's Degree in English Literature from the University of Michigan and a Master's Degree in Counseling. He lives near Detroit with his wife and two daughters.

All Smoke Rises is the second novella featuring Lilly.
Check out Milk-Blood for Lilly's origin story.

Here is the first chapter of Milk-Blood:

CHAPTER ONE: Zachary - *10 am, Day after Christmas*

PUDDLES OF MUD.

After she confessed her eyes became puddles of mud, like tears had fallen upon dirty eye sockets and left a muddy mess.

"Okay, yes, it was Puckett. We had sex," she squeaked. "Three times only. I didn't mean to. Will you still take care of us?"

Latrice only confessed because she was caught. The paternity test showed a 99 percent chance that Zach wasn't the father. She held the child of Puckett in her womb.

"Will you take care of us?" she asked again. It wasn't a question. She was giving him a challenge. He took care of what he loved. His mother had been his to tend to for years, and they both got by with the help of some pills. He would take care of her until one of them died, because that's what he did. But Latrice with another man's child inside of her?

"I will take care of things," he answered, but he didn't say the rest that he wanted to, which was, *"Because the day I fucked you I caught an infection and now I have it for life."*

"What about Puckett? Will you do him like you usually do?"

"Yes, I will."

He had to. Because now Puckett has the infection too, and he was sure to come around running his mouth about being the father of Latrice's child.

Puckett spent three more days alive before Zach found him. Suffocation by choking had always been his choice when he wanted others to think for a moment about whose hands were killing them. His hands came alive with power when wrapped around someone's throat. Like squeezing a loaf of soft bread he could squeeze necks, but when his hands were around

Puckett's bulging windpipe, he eased up. He wanted to hear him talk. He wanted a confession. When one didn't come and Puckett played stupid, he squeezed until he saw a shade of blue in Puckett's face and his body danced on the edge of death. Then he relaxed his fingers and let him gasp for air and come back to life. Dipping him in, and pulling him out. He could have done it all day, and nearly did, until the shade of blue seemed to burst and no more air was needed.

Later, Puckett would swim deep. The Detroit River doesn't give up its dead easy, and it was a better option than his burn and bury method. Last time he burned something was when he fire-bombed the house across the street with a Molotov cocktail made of vodka (100 proof). The whole block around Brentwood was rained on with ashes and soot of the boy who died that night. Latrice loved it when she could get into his head and make him kill, except for this time when a boy had died. But now she was giving birth to a new child, a baby girl, to replace him on this street. Spirit in, spirit out.

Labor pains doubled her over in pain a month before her due date, and Zach drove her to the hospital at 4:30 am on a Tuesday. The delivery room was lit like a spaceship and reminded Zach of his trip to Vegas. No windows, no escape, and you won't leave without being changed. He couldn't tell if it was day or night as the hours passed. He slipped out more than once to chew on his own supply of Percocets or Vicodins or Xanax, and came back feeling cleansed each time.

What he saw was a foreign liquid flowing from between Latrice's propped up legs. It smelled of something spoiled being cooked, something ominous—bigger than her, bigger than this hospital could handle. Latrice went inward into silent agony at times, at other times yelled not with words but noises. She dripped sweat, spasmed, and when the head crowned, Zach felt both nauseous bile and warm shivers of hope.

There was a one percent chance that the baby girl would have his ebony flesh. The miracle waited in his chest, thumping, wanting to explode. But on first sight the thump died. She did not. In fact, the baby's flesh was a veiny blue color and so pale it was nearly see-through.

A heart condition kept the child in intensive care for days, in an incubator, looking like a blue frog ready to be dissected. Zach peeked in at her and tried to make eye contact, did make eye contact. This infant seemed to be his very own heart beating in front of him, shriveled and alien, with doctors prodding it to keep it alive.

"She's going to die," Latrice repeated again and again. "I can't take this, I can't see her. You do it, you stay here."

He did, and he slept in the hospital on plastic pillows while Latrice went home to watch over his mother who lived with them on 618 Brentwood Drive.

His lone finger in the sterile glove touched the infant girl's forehead.

Where's my mother? She asked him with tiny motions of her incubated arms.

Soon. Soon you will see her. I am here. This is how it is.

Days later, talking hospital heads gave him instructions and medicine and appointment reminders, and he brought the child home to Latrice. Life had grown stronger in the nameless infant, but she was still barely bigger than the palm of his hand. At home the child shrieked and wailed as if it hurt just to be alive.

"This is not how it's supposed to be," Latrice said, watching Zach holding the wailing child at 3:36 am in the rocker on a Tuesday.

"This is how it's going to be."

He slept with the 10 day old baby flesh on his own. The skin was so thin you could see her insides, like it wasn't fully done growing and she was thrown into the world before her time. Their bodies warmed each other and he rocked her on his chest until 4:25 am. She fell asleep against the beat of his heart.

On her mother's chest, she refused to take the breast and would not sup at the nipple introduced to her mouth. Latrice seemed as scared of the child as the child was of it.

Medications the baby did take. Zach injected them into an IV port in her neck. Warnings from doctors rang in his ears. Too large of an injection could lead to asphyxiation. Failure to administer would do the same. She was already like so many who lived on this street and needed a daily drug to face each day.

Latrice curled up into a ball much of the time. Her hair, unwashed for days, became stringy as a broom. Pill bottles with the prescription labels rubbed off sat on the counter. Oxys or Xanax or both.

The infant tears came at night—sometimes for hours, non-stop. When they got too much and it seemed the child herself might shatter, the parents would wrap themselves in jackets against the cold and take dark trips to the hospital, only to be sent back home again. Sleeplessness weighed them down like soaking wet clothes.

"This isn't how it's supposed to be," she said.

"This is how it is," he answered.

"No. No. You can take care of this. Take care of her like you do. Make it like it was before. She's not meant to be alive." Her eyes filled with tears once again. They pleaded to him. The infection bubbled in his veins.

Killing again would be easy.

He walked around the house, pacing, gaining energy with each stride, summoning up the courage to do the deed. This one needed to be fast and clean, unlike Puckett.

When he held the pillow over her face, he smothered her with his whole body weight to make it quick, but it may not have been needed. Things were fragile already, and they were just tiny breaths to take away this time.

The body fit easily into his trunk, the night air cold around him. The car seats were frigid leather. Soon the car would heat up, and things would be better. He whispered middle of the night words to his passenger in the back seat.

"We're taking mommy to her grave. Then we'll be home. I will name you Lilly, and I will take care of you as long as I live."

My infection is gone, he thought, as he drove with the body ready to burn and bury.

www.ingramcontent.com/pod-product-compliance
Lightning Source LLC
Chambersburg PA
CBHW010939120626
46554CB00008B/2534